THE HARLEM CHARADE

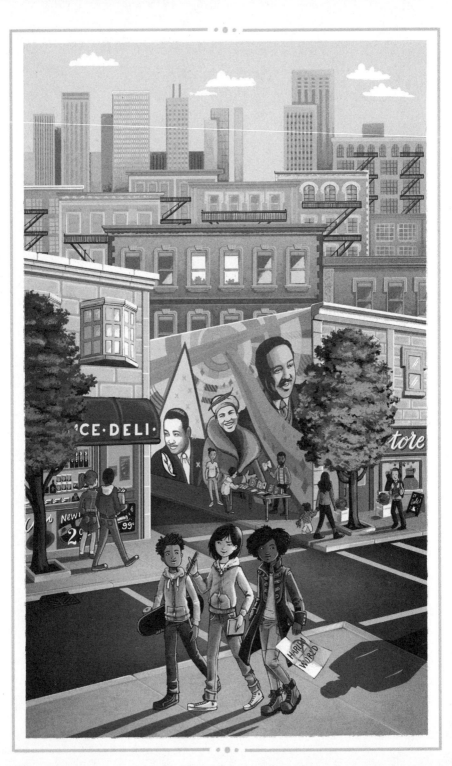

THE
HARLEM
CHARADE

NATASHA TARPLEY

SCHOLASTIC PRESS
NEW YORK

Library of Congress Cataloging-in-Publication Data

Names: Tarpley, Natasha, author. | Title: The Harlem charade / by Natasha Tarpley. Description: First edition. | New York, NY : Scholastic Press, 2017. | Summary: Seventh-graders Jin, Alexandra, and Elvin come from very different backgrounds and circumstances, but they all live in Harlem, and when Elvin's grandfather is attacked they band together to find out who is responsible—and the search leads them to an enigmatic artist whose missing masterpieces are worth a fortune, and into conflict with an ambitious politician who wants to turn Harlem into an historic amusement park. | Identifiers: LCCN 2016040577 | ISBN 9780545783873 (hardcover) | Subjects: LCSH: Detective and mystery stories. | Political participation—Juvenile fiction. | African American artists—Juvenile fiction. | Studio Museum in Harlem—Juvenile fiction. | Community development—New York (State)—New York—Juvenile fiction. | Harlem (New York, N.Y.)—Juvenile fiction. | CYAC: Mystery and detective stories. | Studio Museum in Harlem—Fiction. | African Americans—Fiction. | Community life—New York (State)—Harlem—Fiction. | Political participation—Fiction. | Harlem (New York, N.Y.)—Fiction. | New York (N.Y.)—Fiction. | GSAFD: Mystery fiction. | LCGFT: Detective and mystery fiction. | Classification: LCC PZ7.T176 Har 2017 | DDC 813.54 [Fic] —dc23 LC record available at https://lccn.loc.gov/2016040577

10 9 8 7 6 5 4 3 2 1   17 18 19 20 21

Printed in the U.S.A.   23

First edition, February 2017

Book design by Carol Ly

TO HARLEM, PAST AND FUTURE.

Harlem, with its stately brownstones, honking horns, and bustling street life, passed in a blur as Jin Yi sprinted the entire ten blocks from school to her grandparents' bodega. Her student council meeting had run long, and now she was late. Her friend Rose, who was meeting her at the store to work on their history class project, would be arriving any minute.

Breathless, Jin flung open the heavy front door and rushed inside, where she promptly whacked her knee on the corner of a large box, which was nearly blocking the store's entrance. *Ow, ow, ow!*

"Pretty sure this is a fire code violation!" she yelled to no one in particular.

Normally, the store was neat and orderly. Halmoni could tell if just one can was out of place on the shelf. Jin's grandmother had eyes like an eagle. One Wednesday a month, though, on inventory night, the place turned into a labyrinth of boxes and crates full of new merchandise.

Argh! It was Wednesday. She had completely forgotten about inventory night when she'd invited Rose over to study, and now it was too late to cancel. Jin eyed the stacks of canned vegetables, cereal boxes, and other items waiting to be shelved or stored. Several of her family members usually showed up to help out, but even with the extra hands, she knew they would be here until midnight putting all this stuff away.

Jin sighed as she limped toward the back of the store, her knee still throbbing like crazy. She bent to rub it and nearly toppled over when her aunt, Ye-Eun, who worked in the store some afternoons, suddenly emerged from one of the aisles.

"Careful there, kiddo." She smiled, reaching for Jin's arm to steady her.

"I'm okay," Jin blushed. "I just didn't see you there," she muttered.

"Hard to see anything with all this stuff everywhere. But we'll get it cleared out tonight." She rumpled Jin's shoulder-length black hair. "Oh, and by the way, it's kimchi day!" she announced with a mischievous wink as she breezed out the door. The word *kimchi* was still hanging in the air when Jin smelled it—the undeniable and overpowering spicy odor of fermented cabbage, hot peppers, and fish sauce. On kimchi days, Halmoni lugged large Tupperware containers full of kimchi that she had made days ago at their apartment to the bodega so they could jar it and sell it in the store. Halmoni was pretty famous for her kimchi. It always flew off the shelves, so they were constantly filling jars with the stuff—at least it seemed that way to Jin.

"Ah, Jinnie, you finally here." Halmoni's curly black hair, frizzy from years of home perms, popped up from behind the front counter. "Come help with kimchi."

"My friend Rose is coming over to do homework, remember? Can I help you with the kimchi later? And, Halmoni, can we, um, keep the lid closed tight on the Tupperware for now? I love your kimchi, but I'm not sure Rose has ever tried it before . . ."

Halmoni took a big whiff from the kimchi-filled Tupperware in front of her. "Anybody don't like kimchi, don't need to come to my store." She tossed her head back proudly. "But okay, we do kimchi later. Go and greet Harabeoji now." She shooed Jin away.

"Thanks, Halmoni," Jin said, walking toward the back of the store. She dumped her bag in the storeroom, then poked her head into the tiny office where her grandfather worked. "Hey, Harabeoji! How are you?"

Harabeoji grunted but didn't look up from the papers on his desk. Jin figured he must be doing paperwork for the store, which always made him grumpy. She headed back out front, just as Rose walked through the door.

"Over here!" Jin waved. "Watch out for the boxes," she said as she pushed aside a small stack to clear a path. "It's inventory night."

"I'm used to it. Now that my parents' divorce is official and they've sold our apartment, it's box city at my house, too." Rose shrugged.

"I'm really sorry about your parents." Jin gave Rose a sympathetic smile. "Do you know where you're going to move?"

"Not yet. My mom is looking for a new apartment for us. It must be cool to have your own bodega," Rose changed the subject as she looked around the small store. "Do you get to eat all the chips and the candy bars you want?"

"Not really. My grandparents are pretty strict about junk food. But I'm sure it'll be okay with them if we eat some today." Jin grinned and grabbed a couple of bags of chips from the display near the counter, then led the way to the back room.

As she and Rose passed his office, Harabeoji, who had fallen asleep in his chair, let out a loud wheeze. "Don't mind my grandfather. His snore is worse than his bite," Jin joked, and ducked beneath the clothesline that stretched across the back room, where Halmoni hung her clean aprons, store clothes, and cleaning rags to dry. Jin led Rose to the small table, where she and her grandparents sometimes ate dinner when they were working late at the store. "By the way, hope you don't mind the TV on in the background. Halmoni and Harabeoji like to watch the news." Jin turned down the volume knob on the small old-fashioned television perched on a shelf behind the table.

"No problemo." Rose said, already pulling books out of her bag. "So what are you going to do for your American history project?"

Jin shrugged. Their teacher, Ms. Weir, had assigned a research paper about a historical event or unique quality that had influenced the character of their neighborhood. The paper was worth nearly half of the entire grade for the class. Jin still hadn't figured out her topic, and she was starting to worry. She lived in Harlem, one of the most famous neighborhoods in New York City, in the entire country even. Why was coming up with one good idea so hard?

"I'm tossing around a couple of ideas," Jin said. "I could research the contributions of Korean immigrants like my grandparents, who came to Harlem in the 1960s. Or maybe the Harlem Renaissance? When we studied it in class, I wanted to learn more about the African American writers, musicians, and painters who put Harlem on the map as the place to be for art and culture. But I don't know." Jin sighed. "I just wish Ms. Weir had been a little more specific." She took her schoolwork very seriously and liked her assignments to be clear.

"I think not being specific is kind of the point," Rose said. "Both of your ideas sound awesome. You just have to pick the one that's most interesting to you. I'm going to do my project on Harlem fashion." She flailed her hands in the air excitedly. "I'll track the hottest Harlem styles from the past to the present." Rose pulled out her phone. "And speaking of fashion, check out the new winter collection that I'm designing for Noodles." Noodles was Rose's adorable black-and-tan pug. She loved that dog just as much as she loved clothing. Rose leaned over so that Jin could see the picture of Noodles in a puffy neon green dog-sized coat with matching scarf and hat on the screen.

"Awww. He's so cute!" Jin cooed as Rose rapidly swiped through more photos.

"Oh, and this is from the summer collection." She paused at a picture of Noodles in an old-fashioned one-piece striped bathing suit with a swim cap. "We never go to the beach, but he can wear it to splash around in the fountain at the dog park . . ."

"Mmmm-hmm." Jin's eyes wandered to the television as Rose continued to gush about Noodles. There was a news story on about a local community garden.

"Hey, that's not far from here." Jin turned up the volume as images of the garden flashed across the screen.

"Buried treasure in Harlem? Quite possibly. Yesterday, seven-year-old Harlem resident, Jarvis Monroe, may just have discovered a hidden masterpiece at the Zora Neale Hurston Community Garden," said a reporter, on location in front of the garden. The camera cut to a grungy-looking kid holding a toy sand shovel and pail.

"It was right over there." Jarvis pointed. *"I was visiting my grandma. She lives across the street."* He nodded toward an apartment building in the background. *"She told me not to dig in the garden, but I did it anyway and that's where I found the painting."* The camera zoomed in on a patch of dirt beneath a wooden bench. The reporter asked him to describe what he had found. *"It looked kinda like a rolled-up tube, like the one that's in the middle of a roll of paper towels.*

Except this tube was covered in plastic and the outside was really dirty."

The reporter took a step away from Jarvis as he continued his report. *"Experts believe that Jarvis Monroe may have uncovered a rare painting by a Harlem artist, who, at the beginning of a very promising career in the 1960s, suddenly and mysteriously vanished from the art world along with all her paintings. No definitive information has been released at this time, but if the painting is an original work, it would be one of the most significant art finds of the decade, and worth a lot of money. Not bad for a seven-year-old kid digging in the dirt,"* the reporter joked.

"Wow," said Rose, who had stopped talking about Noodles long enough to listen to the story. "Can you imagine making such a major art discovery at *seven*?"

"That is pretty impressive," Jin said. "Maybe I should do my history project on Jarvis Monroe," she half-joked as she glanced back at the screen, where a man was now standing beside Jarvis, his arm slung awkwardly across the kid's shoulders. The man's name and title, Geld Markum, City Council Member, flashed across the screen. He had a large space in between his front teeth, and when he spoke, the tip of his tongue poked through the gap. He reminded Jin of a snake.

"*That's why my Harlem World project is so important. We need to preserve the history and culture of Harlem, including works of art like the one our little man, Jarvis, here has uncovered. Otherwise, they just disappear. Right, Jarvis?*" Councilman Markum broke into a broad grin and gripped Jarvis's shoulder as the boy tried to inch away.

"*We expect widespread community support—*" Councilman Markum was saying when, suddenly, a wet rag slammed against the television screen with a loud *splat!* Jin and Rose turned to see who had thrown the rag. Halmoni stood scowling behind them.

"That man no good, like poison. He going to ruin neighborhood!" Halmoni stormed over to the television, switched it off, and wiped up the water with the same rag she had just thrown.

"Are you, uh, okay, Halmoni?" Jin asked hesitantly. Her grandmother always had a temper, but Jin had never seen her throw anything.

"I'm fine. Better now I don't see Markum's face." Halmoni let out a deep breath. "Jin, I need you out front. The produce man is here, and I have to watch him. Last time, he try cheat me out of five pounds of bananas." Halmoni stomped back to the front of the store.

Rose stood to leave. "I should get going anyway. My mom freaks if I stay out too late," she said.

"I hope Halmoni didn't scare you off," Jin said as she led Rose to the door.

"Please! She's a softy compared to my nana. See you at school tomorrow." Rose waved as she slipped past Halmoni, who was arguing bananas with the produce guy at the door.

Jin watched her grandmother haggle. Halmoni seemed so sure of where she stood on things, first with that city councilman, now with the banana man. If only Jin had inherited some of that conviction. Then maybe she'd already have a topic for her history project.

Jin wandered back to the counter to watch the register while Halmoni went outside with the deliveryman to open the basement's sidewalk entrance. Jin hated going down there; it was dark and damp and creepy, and she always half expected to trip over some random skeleton sticking out from a dark corner. *That* was one discovery she did *not* want to make. She shuddered as she scooted onto the stool behind the cash register. She plunked her elbows onto the counter and rested her chin in her hands.

Why was Halmoni so upset about that Markum guy? Jin's thoughts drifted as she stared out at the empty store. After a few minutes, she slid off the stool to check the candy display. It was her job to make sure it was well stocked. She noticed right away that they were running low on Kit Kat bars and Wint O Green Life Savers. She took another quick glance around the store and ducked into the back to grab more candy. When she returned to the register, there was a man in the store. Jin hadn't even heard him come in.

"Uh, hello," she called out to the customer. The man, who was wearing a long black trench coat and a Harlem Black Bombers baseball hat nodded in her direction. When he turned toward her, Jin could see that he was an older man, maybe in his sixties, with a scruffy white beard that stood out against his light brown skin, and small, round wire-frame glasses. *Now, what's his story?* she wondered, pretending to be busy with the candy display so that she could watch him without being too obvious. Halmoni always said that, being in the grocery business, you have to know what people are hungry for at the moment, and you also have to remind them what they're really craving—that is, what they really truly need and want in their lives.

What was this man hungry for? Jin was all set to guess, when the man quickly picked up a package of spaghetti and a jar of pasta sauce. *No fair! You didn't give me time to guess,* Jin wanted to say as he laid his selections on the counter. Instead, she just smiled and rang up his items. "That'll be four dollars and eight cents," she said.

The man started fishing around in his huge coat pocket. "Oh, and I'll take that, too."

Jin followed his eyes to the top shelf of the candy display, where Halmoni kept all the exotic candy from countries like Poland, Korea, India, and China. She also kept a collection of Pez dispensers up there, except she didn't have any of the popular superhero or cartoon character ones. No, Halmoni's Pez dispensers were all random animals, or corny holiday-themed ones, like pumpkins or Easter bunnies. They almost never sold anything from the top shelf.

"Which one?" Jin asked.

"The goat."

She stood on tippy-toe to reach it. "Are you sure about this?" she asked, handing him the red plastic Pez dispenser, with a goat head perched on top. "You want me to show you how it works?" The old man didn't look like the kind of person who ate a lot of Pez.

"That won't be necessary," he said.

Jin suddenly had another thought. "May I make a suggestion?" she asked. The man nodded. "If you're buying this for a kid, most of the ones that I know would be happier with a chocolate bar."

The man shook his head. "No, this is what I want." He slipped the goat into his pocket, paid for his items, and left as quietly as he had come.

A few minutes later, Halmoni barreled back into

the store. "That produce man always try cheat me, but this time, I got him. I use my own scale, ha!" Halmoni clapped her hands. "It right there in black-and-white. Can't argue with numbers. I tell him I only pay for what scale says I owe. He won't cheat me again. Hmmph! Any customer come in?"

"Just an old man. He bought one of your Pez dispensers," Jin said. Halmoni glanced at the empty space on the shelf.

"The goat," she whispered, and frowned.

"What? Was I not supposed to sell it?" Jin huffed.

"No, is okay," Halmoni said, and changed the subject. "You do homework now, Jinnie, so you can be ready for inventory later."

Yes! Jin cheered to herself, stifling the urge to pump her fist in the air. In a little while, the place would be crawling with aunts, uncles, and cousins who came to help Halmoni and Harabeoji restock the shelves. She loved that her family helped each other out—that was a big thing for them. But being in a small space with so many of her family members talking and laughing loudly could be a smidge over-whelming. Jin was happy to have a few moments of peace and quiet.

She quickly grabbed her backpack from the store-room and retreated to her special place behind the deli display case. Because the store was so small, Jin had nowhere to do homework if she had to help out up front. Harabeoji had created a space for her to work in the small alcove behind the deli case. It was perfect—just big enough for her to fit comfortably. Halmoni had even donated a small rug and fluffy cushion from their apartment to make it cozy. Best of all, Jin could look through the glass window of the case and see the entire store, but no one could see her.

Instead of starting her homework right away, she decided to spend a few minutes observing. Unlike her grandmother, who liked to guess about people's lives, Jin preferred to watch. She was a collector of interesting moments and details. When she wasn't working, Jin's favorite thing to do was to watch the people who came into the store. She'd figured out that, if you pay close attention, people will tell you their stories in the way that they move, how their faces look, how they speak. When something interesting caught her eye about a person or a moment, she wrote it down in her memory notebook so that she could always remember it.

Halmoni believed that maybe Jin saved so many moments because she had a hole in her own memory. Jin was abandoned as a baby. The woman who was her mother had left her in a box at the Korean

Presbyterian Church Halmoni and Harabeoji attended in Queens, then climbed into the wind and disappeared. When her grandparents found out about her arrival, they immediately adopted Jin, and they'd been her family ever since. Jin never learned anything more about her birth mother.

"Moments are like birds," Halmoni always told her. "Not good to keep them caged up in notebook. Let them go." But Jin liked being able to flip through her notebooks and see moments that she'd saved a year or two ago, as if they'd just happened. You never knew when you might need to remember a specific detail or event. Maybe she would even make an important discovery like Jarvis Monroe did, finding that painting in the garden.

She glanced up at the two round mirrors perched like eyeballs near the ceiling. They allowed a view of all five of the store's aisles at once, and right now reflected the image of a strange-looking girl walking into the store. She wove around the stacks of boxes and slunk down the condiment aisle. Jin couldn't really see her face but noticed that the girl had reddish-brown skin and dark, shoulder-length hair cut into a choppy, uneven style. She wore a long black jacket held together with safety pins instead of buttons and clunky combat boots. Jin grabbed her pale pink notebook and started writing as fast as she could:

> She walks slightly hunched over, like she doesn't want to draw attention to herself. Her eyes keep darting around. What is she looking for? What is she hiding?

Jin continued to watch as the girl paced from aisle to aisle, pausing briefly to look at one item or another. At one point, she stopped and stared squarely into one of the mirrors near the ceiling. Jin gasped. She knew this girl! She was in her history class at school, but she couldn't remember the girl's name. Jin wondered whether she should go over to say hello, to be polite, but she really just wanted to watch a little while longer.

A few seconds later, the girl returned to the condiment aisle. She pulled a small object out of her pocket and stuck it onto one of the jars on the shelf. As Jin strained to see what it was, her uncle Jae's gigantic head appeared on the other side of the deli case, obstructing her view.

"Surprise! Whatcha looking at, Jinnie Bean?"

Uncle Jae exclaimed as he bobbed from side to side, playfully blocking her as she desperately stretched her neck to see around him.

"Nothing." Jin frowned, scuttling out from behind the deli case. By the time she got to the condiment aisle, the girl was gone. Jin quickly scanned the shelves to try to find what the girl had left there. And then she saw it. Taped to a jar of dill pickles was a MetroCard subway pass with a pink smiley face Post-it note that said *Enjoy 1 Free Ride.* Jin stuffed the card and the note into her pocket, and before she even knew what she was doing, she was heading toward the storeroom to grab her jacket. She had to follow this girl.

"Back in a little while," Jin yelled as she zipped past Halmoni and Harabeoji.

"Where you go? We do inventory soon," Halmoni called after her.

"Research!" Jin called as she sailed through the door, glimpsing another MetroCard and note nestled among the apples in the bin near the entrance.

On the sidewalk in front of the store, Jin realized that she had no idea where she was going. Her family's bodega was on 125th and Malcolm X Boulevard, which was a pretty crowded intersection. *How am I ever going to find her with all these people around?* Jin frantically looked up and down the block, her heart beating like a wild bird in her chest. The girl was nowhere in sight.

She was about to give up when she heard a voice say, "Yeah, it was just taped to the chair with a note. A free MetroCard. Isn't that amazing?" She turned to see a man coming out of the coffee shop next door, showing off his find to a friend. That was the clue she needed. Jin took off in the direction of the coffee shop.

After about a block, she saw the girl's choppy hair bobbing up and down in the crowd, a few of the strands waving like fingers. *This way, this way.* The girl's long black jacket blew out behind her like a cape. Jin wished that she had her notebook, but she'd been in such a rush to leave, she'd forgotten it at the store. *I'll just have to remember this on my own,* she thought.

She made sure to keep enough distance between herself and the girl that she wouldn't be seen. They walked east on 125th Street, weaving through throngs of people, dogs, and baby strollers. Along the way, Mystery Girl stopped at random cafés, stores, and bus stops to leave her MetroCards and smiley-face notes.

At one point, she ran out of cards. Jin followed her into a subway station and watched from behind a large man with a huge shopping cart, as Mystery Girl whipped out a credit card and bought a whole bunch more at the vending machine. *A credit card? What kid has her own credit card, let alone enough money to buy all those subway passes?* Jin wondered. Once Mystery Girl had amassed a small stack, she stuck a smiley-face note on each one and headed back out to the street. Jin wanted to keep following her, but she knew that Halmoni and Harabeoji would be expecting her. Reluctantly, she walked back to the store, her mind full of questions.

Who is this girl? What just happened? Jin wasn't really sure. All she knew was that she intended to find out.

The next day in history class, Jin listened closely as Ms. Weir took attendance and found out that Mystery Girl's name was Alexandra Roebuck. *That was disappointing.* She'd assumed that the girl's name would be a little less, well, ordinary.

Alexandra sat at the end of the row in front of Jin's, near the window. She was wearing the same ripped black jacket and combat boots she had on yesterday. *How have I not paid attention to her before?* Jin thought, and quickly reached for her notebook. As she flipped it open, the MetroCard Alexandra had left taped to the pickle jar at the store fluttered out and landed in her lap, a tiny reminder of all the questions she still needed to answer about what had happened yesterday.

Jin glanced at Alexandra, who was staring out the window, twirling a piece of her hair around her finger. Ten minutes later, she was still in the exact same position. Jin began to scribble.

Alexandra is still looking out the window. What is she thinking about? Is she some kind of genius who doesn't have to work as hard as everybody else????

Halfway through the period, Ms. Weir gave the class time to work on their neighborhood projects. Rose, who sat on the other side of the room, dragged her chair over to Jin's desk so they could work together. Jin shot a look in Alexandra's direction. She was still in her seat, staring out the window. After a few seconds, she pulled out a pad of pink Post-it notes, like the one she'd left in the store with the MetroCard, and began to write on them, one at a time. *Maybe she's planning another MetroCard expedition . . .*

"Hey, did you hear me?" Rose nudged Jin.

"Huh?" Jin blinked.

"Your project. I asked if you had picked a topic for your project. What were you staring at anyway?" Rose frowned.

"Nothing. I'm still deciding on my topic. How's yours going?" Jin quickly changed the subject.

"I found the coolest website about fashion during the Harlem Renaissance. Weren't you interested in doing something about the writers and artists during that time?" Rose asked, but didn't give Jin time to answer. "I just adore the 1920s-style dresses with their long waists and beadwork and . . ."

As Rose continued to talk about her idea, Jin's attention drifted back to Alexandra. She was dying to find out what Alexandra had written on her Post-it notes, but how? Maybe she could casually walk by her desk and just *happen* to sneak a peek.

"Uh, Rose, I've gotta go sharpen my pencil," Jin said. Rose gave her a weird look as Jin grabbed a couple of stubby pencils from her pencil case. She was just about to get up from her desk, when Alexandra suddenly whipped around in her seat with a seriously evil expression on her face. At first, Jin thought that the look was directed at her, but as she followed the direction of Alexandra's gaze, she saw that the death stare was actually intended for Brittany Stevenson, who was blabbing loudly to Camilla Chen about her upcoming birthday party. Jin sat back in her chair.

"I thought you were going to sharpen your pencil," Rose said.

"Changed my mind. I'll use a pen."

"Suit yourself." Rose shrugged. Jin reached for a pen and pretended to take notes for her project as she eavesdropped on Brittany.

"It's going to be sooo cool," Brittany gushed. "My

parents are renting out the entire spa, and everybody is going to get mani-pedis and makeovers. I already know what they're giving me: a new iPhone, diamond earrings, and that gold Prada bag I've had my eye on. Then for the second half of my birthday present, they're taking me to Milan for a shopping spree this summer. Awesome, right?"

Alexandra looked like she wanted to strangle Brittany. When the end-of-period bell rang, she charged over to her and thrust a small white card in her face. "This is an organization that helps needy kids. Maybe you should think about donating some of your *awesome* birthday gifts." Alexandra seethed.

Brittany just scowled, completely ignoring the card. "I feel sorry for those kids, but honestly, it's not my fault that they don't have stuff."

"Yeah, but you do, and you could use your stuff to make their lives better." Alexandra locked eyes with her.

"That's not really my job or my problem."

"It's everyone's problem." Alexandra forced the words out through clenched teeth.

"You're one to talk." Brittany rolled her eyes and packed up her books. "What a weirdo," she snickered to Camilla as they sauntered out of the classroom. Alexandra stormed back to her seat.

Jin's mouth hung open. True, it was really annoying the way Brittany was constantly bragging about being rich, but it seemed like Alexandra took it personally, like Brittany had done something to her specifically. Now Jin really wanted to talk to her, but as she inched her way over to Alexandra's desk, she started to lose her nerve. *Too close to back down now,* she thought as she took a deep breath and lightly tapped her Mystery Girl on the shoulder.

"Hi, Alexandra," she said cheerfully. She wanted to appear friendly but not overly eager.

"It's Alex," the girl answered flatly, stuffing books into her bag without looking up. Jin wasn't sure what to say next, but then she remembered the MetroCard. "I think you dropped this yesterday." She held up the card.

Alex glanced at it with a blank expression on her face. "I didn't drop it."

"Okay, I know you didn't just drop it. But I saw you. My grandparents own the bodega where you left it. You know, on the pickle jar?"

"Okay." Alex shrugged. Awkward silence.

"Um, I think what you did with the MetroCards was really cool. If you do it again, I, uh, I'd like to come with you," Jin stammered. She knew she probably sounded totally desperate, but she didn't care.

"I work alone," Alex said firmly as she swung her bag over her shoulder, heading toward the door.

"Just a moment, Alexandra," Ms. Weir called. Jin went back to her desk and packed up her stuff as slowly as possible so that she could listen to their conversation.

"I'm not sure what's going on, Alex, but we're already a month into the school year and you've turned in less than half of the homework assignments. You're also not doing the work that's required during class time. I haven't seen any evidence that you've even started your neighborhood project, which is worth forty percent of your grade. If you don't complete this project, you're in danger of failing this class, and I don't want that to happen." Ms. Weir had a concerned frown on her face.

Alex just shrugged and stared down at the floor.

"If it's a matter of needing extra help, I'm always available to work with you after school," Ms. Weir offered. Alex didn't say anything. "Okay, well, this neighborhood project is your best chance to make up the work that you've missed. If you do well, you'll be in good shape to pass. Perhaps it would help to work with another student? You're allowed to work in groups."

Alex grunted. "I prefer to work by myself."

"However you choose to do it is up to you. But I need you to know how important this project is. Do you understand?" Ms. Weir asked.

"Yes, I get it! May I be excused now?" Alex huffed.

Ms. Weir handed Alex an envelope. "Please give this to your parents. I'd like to speak with them."

Alex grabbed the envelope and rushed toward the door. Jin cornered her before she could make it out of the classroom.

"I wasn't eavesdropping—"

"Sure about that?" Alex interrupted.

Jin blushed but continued. "I heard what Ms. Weir said, and I can help with your, uh, situation."

"I don't need your help." Alex clenched her teeth.

Suddenly, Jin had an idea. "Excuse me, Ms. Weir?" The teacher looked up from her desk. "Would it be okay if Alex and I work together on our neighborhood project?" she asked sweetly.

"What are you doing?" Alex hissed. Jin ignored her.

"That would be wonderful!" Ms. Weir beamed. "Alex, what do you say?"

Alex glared at Jin. "Fine," she answered.

Outside in the hall, Alex charged at Jin, leaning so close, their faces were just inches apart. Jin took a step back.

"I don't appreciate being railroaded," Alex said gruffly.

"I just wanted to help," Jin said. Alex let out a loud, angry laugh.

"Yeah, right. What do you really want?"

"I—I want to come with you on one of your missions," Jin said, her voice shaking slightly. Alex didn't say anything for a few seconds, then jabbed her finger toward Jin, stopping just short of her forehead.

"One time," she said. "You can come with me one time. Then you help me with this stupid project, and we're done. I'll meet you at the bodega on Saturday." With that, Alex whirled around and headed down the corridor. Jin saw her crumple up the envelope Mrs. Weir had given her and toss it in the trash.

"Are you okay?" asked Rose, who rushed toward Jin as she was coming back from her locker. "What was that all about?"

"I'm fine. Alex and I just decided to work together on our neighborhood project." Jin grinned, pleased. She was going on a Mystery Girl mission.

Rose frowned. "Why are you smiling? And why would you want to work with that girl? She is totally strange, and possibly dangerous, though she does have good taste in fashion."

"What do you mean? Her clothes are all ripped up and worn-out-looking," Jin said, confused.

"Only because she made them look like that. Believe me, I know my designers. That jacket and those boots? All high-end European designers. Her outfit probably cost two thousand dollars, easy. The real question is why someone would want to ruin such beautiful clothing. It's an insult to designers everywhere," Rose clucked, shaking her head. "Anyhoo, I've gotta get to math. Later!"

"Yeah, see you." Jin waved absently, thinking about what Rose had just told her. If Alex was wearing a two-thousand-dollar outfit, then why was she so angry at Brittany for bragging about her expensive stuff? Jin took out her notebook and wrote:

Things with Alex are getting weird, very weird.
Let's just say, she really is a mystery girl. And
did I really just force her to work with me on our
neighborhood project so that I could hang out with
her on one of her missions? So not like me. What's
up with that?

Saturday afternoon, Jin rushed through her chores at the store and then crawled into her workspace behind the deli case with her memory notebook to jot down a few thoughts before Alex arrived. Jin wanted to make sure they came up with a subject for their class project today. She also had a million questions that she wanted to ask Alex about herself—even though she was almost certain Alex wouldn't want to answer them. Still, it was better to be prepared in any case.

"You finish homework?" Halmoni, who was perched on the stool behind the cash register, eyed her suspiciously.

"I finished it yesterday," Jin answered, biting the end of her pen. She was just about to start writing when the door to the bodega flew open. She sucked in her breath and looked up expectantly. It was just Rose. Jin sighed, then felt a twinge of guilt that she was disappointed.

Rose made a beeline to the deli case

and urgently tapped on the glass. "Jin, are you back there? I need to talk to you."

Jin clambered out from behind the counter. Rose's normally pale face was bright red and streaked with tears. "Rose, what happened?" She quickly moved closer and put a hand on Rose's shoulder.

"I'm going to lose Noodles!" Rose wailed. Halmoni calmly handed her a Kleenex.

"What do you mean, lose Noodles?" Jin asked, but Rose was crying too hard to answer, her face getting redder by the second. Jin worried that she might pass out. After a few minutes, Rose calmed down enough to eke out a few words in between sniffles.

"My mom just signed a lease on a new apartment." She gulped for air. "And the building doesn't allow dogs! My dad's new place doesn't, either. It's bad enough that they're getting divorced, now I have to get rid of Noodles, too!" She started to wail again.

"No way! We have to fix this," Jin said, upset now herself. Rose without Noodles just seemed . . . wrong. "I can help you find a new home for Noodles. And we could ask the new owner to allow you to visit him as part of the deal," she volunteered before she had a chance to think it through.

"Really? That's a great idea, Jin! Thank you,

thank you, thank you!" Rose gushed, and gave her friend a big hug. "So how do we do it?"

Jin led her to the back of the store and sat down at the table. "Maybe we could make a flyer." She started sketching out ideas in her notebook. "And I could ask Halmoni to post it on the bulletin board in the store."

"That's brilliant!" A look of relief spread across Rose's face. "Do you mind if I use your computer? I can design a flyer and add a really cute picture of Noodles. It'll only take a few minutes," she suggested.

"Good idea," Jin agreed, and signed her onto the computer in Harabeoji's office. Now, all she had to do was to get Halmoni to agree to the plan, which could be easier said than done. Halmoni was pretty strict about what she posted on the store's community bulletin board. One time, she refused to post a flyer for someone selling a car because she thought they were charging too much. Jin had given up trying to figure out her grandmother. She remembered reading somewhere once that the best way to persuade someone to do something was to give them enough options so that they couldn't say no. While Rose worked on the computer, Jin wrote out a list of options to present to Halmoni:

OPTION ONE: Ask if we can adopt Noodles. The answer is likely to be no, so proceed to

OPTION TWO: Ask if we know anyone in the family, or from the store who wants a dog. If no, proceed to

OPTION THREE: Can we post a flyer in the store?

By the time Jin finished her list, Rose had designed a flyer that featured the cutest picture of Noodles dressed in a little three-piece tweed suit. They printed out a few copies so that Rose could post them around the neighborhood and brought one to the front of the store to show Halmoni. Jin went through her list of options. Halmoni said no to the first two, but when she asked her if she would post the flyer on the bulletin board, Halmoni said yes right away.

"This dog look very professional. I like that," Halmoni nodded as she stuck the flyer up on the board.

Rose flung herself at Halmoni, hugging her tightly. "Thank you, Halmoni! Thank you!" She said, tearing up.

"Okay, enough. You welcome." Halmoni pried

Rose off her and shooed her out of the store before she started to cry again.

The door hadn't even closed behind Rose all the way, when Alex walked in, lugging a shopping cart full of groceries behind her. She didn't say anything to Jin, who was standing near the entrance. Instead, she marched right up to the counter and held out her hand for Halmoni to shake.

"Hello, my name is Alex Roebuck, and I'm collecting food donations for the Harlem women's shelter. I was wondering if you would like to make a donation," she said sweetly. Halmoni studied her for a moment before grabbing a couple of plastic bags and quickly filling them with fruit and vegetables from the produce bins. She even added a jar of her prized kimchi.

"No way!" Jin gasped, and quickly clapped her hand over her mouth. Halmoni *never* gave *anything* away without asking questions first. Her grandmother was full of surprises today.

"Thank you so much." Alex smiled as she loaded the bags into her cart. She looked nothing like the scowling angry girl who had unleashed her wrath on Brittany Stevenson in class the other day.

Unfortunately, the old Alex was back by the time

she turned around to face Jin. "Coming?" she hissed, heading toward the door.

"Halmoni, is it okay if I go out with Alex for a little while? She goes to my school and we're working on a project together," Jin asked quietly. She was a little embarrassed that she had to ask to go out, especially in front of Alex, who didn't seem like she had to ask permission to do anything.

"Why you whisper? Speak up!" Halmoni yelled. *Geez, could she be any louder?* Jin's cheeks burned as she took a quick look behind her. Alex had already left.

"I said, is it okay if I hang out with Alex?" *Comeoncomeoncomeon* . . . Jin hopped from one foot to the other.

"Be back before five o'clock," Halmoni instructed. Jin grabbed her jacket and notebook, and sped out the door.

Alex hadn't gotten far with her heavy shopping cart. Jin easily spotted her swerving through the throngs of Saturday shoppers on 125th Street and fell into step beside her.

"Hey, doing a little grocery shopping?" Jin cringed at her corny line, but it was the first thing that came to mind.

Alex was not amused. "Let's get one thing clear." She stopped walking. "You are only here because you pretty much forced me to work with you."

"About that, I've never done—" Jin attempted to explain, but Alex cut her off.

"We are not friends. And us hanging out like this? Not. Happening. Ever. Again. Got it?"

Jin nodded hesitantly. "But isn't it going to be hard to work together if—"

"Oh, and one more thing," Alex cut her off again. "Don't say anything. I do the talking when I make my deliveries. You do not speak to anyone, or touch any of my stuff. Understood?" Again, Jin bobbed her head as they zigzagged through the crowds on 125th Street.

They turned and continued walking uptown. When they stopped at a corner to wait for the light to change, Alex walked over to pet a dog tied to a nearby lamppost. Suddenly, Jin had a brainstorm. Maybe Alex could help her to find a home for Noodles!

"Hey, speaking of helping people," Jin said before the light changed. "My friend Rose, who goes to our school, has to give away her dog, Noodles, because, well, it's a long story. Anyway, I was thinking that maybe you could help us find a new owner?"

"Helping your friend and her stupid dog was not part of our deal," Alex snapped, tugging the cart forward.

"Noodles isn't stupid!" Jin crossed her arms over her chest. "He just needs a new home. You obviously like dogs and I just thought, with all the good deeds you do in the neighborhood, you might know someone."

"I don't."

"Look, I think it's cool that you give MetroCards and food to total strangers. But what about helping a real person, I mean, like someone you might actually know?" For a second, Jin thought she saw the beginnings of a smile as Alex studied her.

"You are very persistent and very annoying. Kind of like a mosquito." Alex shook her head. "I'll keep my eyes open. That's it."

"Awesome! Rose will be so happy." Jin grinned. Alex rolled her eyes. Not to be deterred, Jin kept talking. "Why don't we discuss our project?" she suggested. "We absolutely don't have to do this, but one idea that I had was to do something on the writers and artists of the Harlem Renaissance. Their work really—"

"No offense, but the Harlem Renaissance is *over*," Alex interrupted, shaking her head. "I personally don't see the point of doing something about the past, when so much is going on in Harlem right now." Alex lugged her cart in the direction of a restaurant called the Magic Skillet, located on the corner of 135th and Malcolm X Boulevard.

"So enlighten me. What's going on in Harlem? I live here, too, you know," Jin bristled as she followed Alex into the small diner that was so packed with customers all the windows were fogged. The smell of crisp bacon and grilled hamburgers clinging to the thick air made her stomach grumble.

"Well, for one thing, this restaurant is an institution," Alex said to Jin over her shoulder. "Lots of famous people ate here, including Malcolm X and Dr. Martin Luther King, Jr. But haven't you noticed all the big corporations and restaurant chains that have invaded Harlem recently? Those places almost always push out the poor and the small businesses that serve everyday people. The Magic Skillet may not be around for much longer." Alex scanned the crowd, craning her neck to see over the backs and heads of the diners at the counter.

"It seems like it's doing okay," Jin commented.

"Just a matter of time," Alex said.

"What's that supposed to mean?" Jin asked, but Alex was already moving in the direction of a waitress who was waving at her from the back of the restaurant.

"There you are, sugar!" The woman gave Alex a quick hug with one arm, while pouring coffee with the other. "Got some good stuff for you today." She sat the coffeepot down on a warmer and disappeared into the back. She returned carrying a large shopping bag full of food, and one long French baguette.

"This is great!" Alex stuffed the bag and the bread into her cart. "The women at the shelter are going to love this."

"And here's a little something special for you." The waitress handed her a brown bag with grease stains seeping through paper. "Eat 'em while they're warm," she winked.

"Thanks!" Alex grinned and dragged her cart toward the exit. "Here, try this." She thrust the bag toward Jin once they were out on the street. "Homemade doughnuts. They're the best."

Jin reached in, grabbed a warm doughnut, and took a bite. The outer crust was just the right amount of crispy, and the inside was so fluffy and moist it practically melted on her tongue. She closed her eyes to savor the deliciousness and had another brainstorm.

"We could do our project on small businesses in Harlem!" Her lids flew open. "Or maybe even on the things you're doing to make the neighborhood a better place."

"Uh, I don't know." Alex hesitated. "The things I do are private. I don't like to publicize them. But the small business idea has potential," she said as they turned and headed west on 135th Street.

"I don't get it," Jin said, struggling to keep up with Alex. "People seem to appreciate what you do. If it were me, I would want as many people as possible to know. Wait . . ." Jin paused mid-thought. "What if it wasn't only you? We could interview all sorts of people who are doing good things for Harlem. Like that kid, Jarvis Monroe, who discovered that rare painting."

"Yeah, I heard about that," Alex said.

Jin continued. "Or Councilman Markum and his Harlem World project. What do you know about him?"

Alex stopped abruptly and whirled around. "Never say that man's name around me. Ever," she spat with a scowl, just like the one Halmoni had on her face after she threw the wet rag at the TV. *What's up with this guy? What did he do to make Alex and Halmoni so upset?* Jin wondered. But before she could ask, a kid on a skateboard with a messenger bag slung across his back suddenly swerved in front of them. He made a figure eight around them, then tapped Alex on the head as he passed.

"Hey!" Jin yelled, shocked. She expected Alex to run after him, but instead Alex started laughing and waving. The kid circled back and hopped off his board, flipping it up into his hand. He was tall and skinny, with electric-purple-and-blue dreadlocks, which looked even brighter against his mahogany skin.

"This is my friend Rad." Alex grinned as she introduced him. "And this is Jin."

"What up?" Rad held out his fist to Jin for a bump. Jin tapped it lightly. Rad turned to Alex. "Dude, where you off to?"

"Just making deliveries. You?"

"Gonna start a new piece. I found this killer location and some sick new colors." He opened the flap of his bag to reveal several cans of spray paint. Jin gasped.

"Nice." Alex nodded.

"Total righteousness." Rad nodded back, climbing back on his board "That's why I gotta keep it movin'. Don't wanna lose the light. Later, dudes," he said, pushing off.

"See you at SEEL!" Alex called after him.

"Arf! Arf!" Rad clapped his hands together and

barked like a seal, as he sped down the sidewalk, weaving his way among the pedestrians.

"What was that all about? Are you two in some kind of marine animal club?" Jin's brain buzzed with questions.

"No, it's not *seal*, it's *S-E-E-L,* which stands for the Society for Excellence in Education and Leadership. It's just some stupid club our parents made us join. It's supposed to mold promising young people into the 'leaders of the future,'" Alex said, sarcastically, making air quotations around the words *leaders of the future.*

"Sounds cool."

"Believe me, it's not," Alex replied in a way that made it clear she was done talking about SEEL.

Jin, still curious about Alex's friend Rad, decided to take a different approach. "Is your friend a graffiti artist?"

"Is this an inquisition?" Alex bristled. "If you must know, Rad is an artist. Period. Graffiti is just one of the styles he works in." Alex stopped her cart in front of a plain brick building.

"What's this place?" Jin asked.

"It's the shelter we've been collecting food for," Alex answered as she lifted a few bags out of the cart. Jin reached out to help. "I got it." Alex jerked the bags away. "You stay and watch the cart. And pay attention."

"Yeah, okay." Jin looked away, her feelings a little hurt. "I think I can watch a stupid cart," she snorted under her breath. As Alex marched up to a door on the side of the building, Jin noticed the French baguette sticking up from inside the cart. "You forgot the bread!" she called and held up the loaf, but Alex didn't hear. "Now who's messing up?" she muttered, stuffing the bread back into the cart.

Jin took out her notebook as soon as Alex disappeared inside the shelter.

At a women's shelter. Alex is delivering food. Pretty cool, but still not sure why she does it. What's her deal? BTW, Alex is very bossy and has some strange friends. We just met one kid who does graffiti—which is illegal!!!

We still don't have an idea for our project. Working with her is going to be harder than I thought . . .

Jin was so busy writing that she didn't notice an odd figure, dressed in an oversized trench coat and baseball hat, staring at her from behind a nearby tree. Out of the corner of her eye, she saw a flash of movement and looked up just in time to see the stranger, coat flapping in the air like a pair of giant wings, charge toward her. He slowed down just enough to grab the knobby end of the baguette and lift it out of the cart, leaving only its white paper wrapping behind.

J in let out a small cry of alarm, and Alex came running up beside her.

"Stop, thief!" Alex shouted. The two girls took off after him. As they ran, Jin noticed something tumble out of the stranger's pocket. She rushed ahead to pick it up.

"Hey! Come back! You dropped something!" Jin yelled after him, bending over, hands on knees, to catch her breath. She took a closer look at the object. It was a red plastic Pez candy dispenser with a goat head on top. She knew this goat! It was identical to the Pez dispenser that the old man with the baseball hat had bought in the bodega a few days ago.

"We'll never catch him. He's too fast," Alex wheezed when she caught up with Jin, nearly collapsing beside her. "Hey, what's that?" She snatched the Pez dispenser out of Jin's hand.

"Hey, you!" Alex shouted after the thief, holding the goat above her head. "If you don't get back here with our bread, the goat's toast!"

The figure slowed to a stop and paused for a moment before turning and walking back toward them.

"Why'd you let him steal the bread, anyway?" Alex said out of the corner of her mouth, keeping her eyes steeled on the thief.

"I—I didn't *let* him. He just appeared . . . out of nowhere . . . It happened so fast!" Jin sputtered, her heart pounding against her rib cage as the figure approached. He held his head down so that she couldn't see his face. She wasn't sure who they would find beneath that huge trench coat and baseball hat. She sucked in her breath and stood as tall she could, trying to at least look as brave as Alex, who, with her arms folded across her chest, seemed ready for just about anything.

Close up, the thief wasn't all that scary. He was a full head shorter than both Alex and Jin, who were about the same height. Looking closely at the face peeking out from under the hat, Jin could tell he was just a kid.

"Here's your stupid bread." Without looking up at them, he shoved the baguette toward Alex, who promptly took it and placed it back into the cart.

Jin raised her eyebrows. "I need to talk to you. Now!" she said through clenched teeth, and pulled Alex by a ratty sleeve behind a parked SUV. "I can't believe you actually took the bread back!" Jin admonished. "Did you ever stop to think that maybe he *needs* it? Maybe he's really hungry."

"Yeah, but he could've asked." Alex crossed her arms again.

Jin shook her head. "I thought you wanted to help people. Is this helping people?"

"No, but . . . fine!" Alex spun on her heels, marched back to the cart, and thrust the loaf of bread toward the kid. "Here, keep it."

He hesitated for a second but then shook his head. "No thanks. I just want my goat back."

Jin shot a look at Alex and nodded toward the kid. Alex reluctantly handed over the goat. "If you don't mind me asking, where did you get this dispenser?" Jin asked.

"None of your business," the kid said gruffly, stuffing the goat back into his coat pocket.

"It's just that a man came into my grandparents' grocery store the other day, and he bought one just like it. Now that I think about it, he was dressed almost exactly like you," Jin quickly added.

"What did the guy look like?" The kid gave her a suspicious look.

"He had smooth, light brown skin, a white beard, I remember that, and tiny round glasses."

The kid took a tentative step forward and opened his mouth to speak but just as quickly changed his mind. "Probably just a coincidence," he sighed, and stepped back.

"Maybe not," Jin pressed. This kid was hiding something, and she wanted to find out what. "Just one more question," she ventured, thinking fast. "Did you happen to have spaghetti for dinner a couple nights ago?"

The boy's stomach grumbled loudly.

"I'll take that as a yes." Jin grinned as his stomach grumbled again. "The man who came into the store bought spaghetti and a jar of sauce, which I happen to know is the least flavorful brand that we sell. It probably tasted like tomato-flavored water. Sorry about that."

The kid cracked a smile.

"My name's Jin. What's yours?"

"I'm Elvin," he answered shyly.

Jin nudged Alex to introduce herself. "I don't talk to thieves," Alex said coolly.

Elvin's smile disappeared. "I'm not a thief." He locked eyes with Alex.

"Then what's your deal? I hope you don't steal bread from strangers just for fun."

Alex kept her arms folded across her chest and

tapped her toe against the sidewalk. Jin glanced back and forth between Alex and Elvin, unsure of what to do next. She wanted to know more about Elvin's story, too, and part of her wished she had been the one brave enough to ask the question, but did Alex have to be so rude about it? Elvin looked really uncomfortable, like he wanted to disappear into that coat of his, which was already about ten sizes too big.

Jin took pity on him. "You don't have to answer that," she said, shooting an icy stare in Alex's direction.

"He's my grandfather," Elvin blurted out. "The man who came into your store." His eyes darted nervously in Jin's direction. "He's my grandfather, and he was attacked last Wednesday. Since then, I've been trying to find out what happened." His voice dropped to a whisper as he fished around in his coat pocket and pulled out a folded newspaper clipping, which he passed to Jin.

" 'Man Found Unconscious in Harlem Community Garden,' " Jin read the headline aloud. " 'A man identified as Harlem resident, Jacob Morrow, was found unconscious in the Zora Neale Hurston Community Garden around 3:00 a.m. Thursday morning.' " Jin looked up. "Okay, this is really bizarre. That's the same garden where Jarvis Monroe found the painting, literally a day before."

"What painting?" Elvin asked.

But Jin was too busy skimming the rest of the article to answer. " 'Authorities believe that Morrow, who is currently being treated for head injuries at Harlem Hospital, was wounded late Wednesday night. Police are still investigating the incident. There are no suspects in custody,' " she finished reading, and looked up at Elvin. "What was your grandfather doing in the garden, anyway?"

"That's what I need to figure out," Elvin said.

Jin shot him a worried look. "Maybe you should go to the police."

"No! No police!" Elvin shouted. "They'll take me away. Nobody will know where I am and I'll never find out what happened to my grandfather."

"He's right." Alex frowned.

"So you're out here all alone?" Jin asked, wide-eyed. She'd never met a homeless kid before. Elvin nodded, eyes on the ground. He obviously wasn't ready to tell them his whole life story yet.

"We need to find you a place to stay." Alex started pacing. "But first, you probably need something hot to eat. We could go back to the Magic Skillet," she suggested.

Jin had a better idea. "Let's go to the bodega. I've got to be back soon anyway. Halmoni should be starting dinner by now. She makes a ton of food because our relatives are always dropping by and they're always hungry."

Elvin hesitated. "I'm not sure. I don't usually go places with strangers. I mean, we just met and all."

"We're not ax murderers," Alex joked.

"Yeah, okay, I'll go," he agreed. *If anything happened, I could always outrun them,* he thought to himself.

"Then it's settled." Alex nodded. They headed in the direction of the bodega, the rattle of Alex's cart thudding along the sidewalk the only sound between them. Dusk swept away the last crumbs of sun, making the pleasantly crisp late-September air feel downright frigid. Instinctively, they veered toward one another, forming a three-person barrier against the cold. Jin matched her stride to Elvin's.

"You know," she whispered, "I think your grandfather bought the goat especially for you."

CHAPTER 6

Halmoni was sweeping out front when they arrived at the bodega. Jin cringed when she saw that her grandmother was wearing her "store clothes": a faded smock with an ugly flower pattern, a ratty green sweater, and hideous brown sandals with white socks. She wished that her grandmother could be a little more fashionable, but then she looked at Alex with her ripped-up clothes and Elvin in his oversized coat, and she realized that they probably hadn't even noticed Halmoni's outfit.

"Hey, Halmoni," Jin greeted her. "These are my friends."

Halmoni didn't answer. Instead, she reached for her glasses, which dangled from a chain around her neck, and slipped them onto her face. "Who are you?" She squinted and pointed at Elvin.

Jin blushed. "This is Elvin, and you met Alex earlier. They're going to hang out for a little while, if that's okay. And also we're starving. Could you, uh, maybe make us something to eat?"

"When my work finished? When

someone cook something to eat for me?" Halmoni fussed. She pointed her broom at Alex. "I already give her food today."

Alex tugged at her hair and shifted her weight. Jin could tell she was uncomfortable and rushed to her defense. "Yes, but she donated it to a shelter. And Elvin . . ." She paused when, out of the corner of her eye, she saw Alex mouthing the word no. Jin swallowed, trying to think of something to say. "Um, Elvin's just hungry." She shot Alex a look, which Alex answered with a very quick nod.

Halmoni frowned suspiciously. "You three lucky I'm so generous. I make something. Go sit at the table," she said, and waved them away.

Jin led her small entourage to the back of the store. "Have a seat." She gestured toward the card table and three folding chairs.

Alex parked her cart against the wall and flopped into a chair. "It must be cool to live in a bodega," she commented, glancing around the room at Halmoni's clothesline, sagging with towels and aprons, the stack of plates and glasses on top of a small refrigerator, and the television blaring out the news.

"We don't live here. My grandparents *own* this store. We work late, so we keep some stuff here," Jin snipped.

"Okay, okay, no big deal." Alex held up her hands, as if she were the one being attacked.

As the girls argued, Elvin shook off his huge coat and folded it over the back of one of the remaining chairs. Before he sat down, he peeled off the baseball hat. Spikey, ear-length dreadlocks sprang out around his head.

Jin looked at him, amazed. "Without your coat and hat, you look like a normal kid," she said before she could stop herself.

"Uh, thanks, I guess," Elvin mumbled, taking a seat.

Alex leaned forward. "So what are you? Nine, ten years old?" She asked. Elvin's brown face turned a deep shade of crimson.

"I'm twelve. In the seventh grade." He winced. "I just happen to be a little short for my age," he glared at Alex. "Has anyone ever told you that you ask really rude questions?"

"Good one, Elvin!" Jin raised her hand for Elvin to high-five.

"What is this? Everyone-gang-up-on-Alex day?" Alex swiveled in her chair to turn her back to the table.

"No gang up on anybody at my table." Halmoni appeared at that moment, carrying a tray loaded with

three bowls of rice, each with a fried egg and a generous dollop of kimchi on top. As Elvin sniffed his
bowl, Jin let out a low groan.

"It's fermented cabbage," she explained, anticipat-
ing the question that everyone asked when presented
with Halmoni's specialty.

"Yeah, I know. I love kimchi!" He grinned. "One
of our neighbors back in California used to make it
for my mom and me." He shoved a huge bite into
his mouth. "So how do you two know each other?"
he asked in between mouthfuls.

"We go to the same school," Jin explained. "We're
seventh graders, too," she added.

Alex sat up in her chair and pushed her bowl
aside. "Let's get down to business, shall we?" She
folded her hands on the table and fixed her gaze on
Elvin. "What's your real story? Start from the beginning, and don't leave anything out."

Okay, here goes, Elvin thought as he shifted in
his chair and cleared his throat. "My mom is sick.
Cancer." The words felt heavy and sharp as they fell
from his mouth and sank in the air like clunky chunks
of metal.

"Elvin, I'm so sorry." Jin reached across the table
to touch his arm.

"Me too," Alex mumbled.

Elvin nodded but kept on with his story. If he was going to get this out, it would be now or never. "Three weeks ago, my mom had to go into the hospital for treatment. We don't really have any other family in Berkeley, where I'm from, so she sent me here to stay with my grandfather until she gets better. I'd never met him, never even knew I had a grandfather before that."

He told them how, last Wednesday night, he had heard his grandfather going out for his nightly walk around eleven o'clock. "I was already in bed, so I just went back to sleep. I woke up again around two a.m. to get some water, and my grandfather still wasn't home, which was strange. His walks usually only took an hour or so—"

"Sorry to interrupt." Jin raised her hand as if she were in class. "Do you mind if I take a few notes?" she asked.

"Okay." Elvin shrugged. Jin grabbed her notebook, opened to a new page, and quickly wrote:

ELVIN'S GRANDFATHER'S ATTACK

Clues:
1. Nightly Walk 11 pm. 1 hour.
2. Wednesday: Went out for walk. Probably attacked in garden before midnight.

When she was finished, she nodded at Elvin to continue.

"Like I was saying, I thought my grandfather not coming home was really weird, and I kind of started freaking out. I didn't want to end up by myself in this city, so I decided to go out to look for him. I probably should've thought that idea through a little more carefully, because I didn't even grab a jacket. I also left my phone and keys in the apartment, so I couldn't get back in, which is how I ended up homeless and cold on the streets of New York—the exact thing I didn't want to happen." Elvin sighed, and then continued.

"Luckily, when I got outside, the super from the building next door was putting the trash out. I asked him about my grandfather, and he told me that he sometimes sees him walking near the garden next to the senior citizens' apartment building. I rushed over there and saw something at the entrance that looked like a pile of old clothes, or maybe a few bags of trash. I went over to get a closer look. It was my grandfather, and he was barely conscious. I yelled for help, and this man who was out walking his dog called an ambulance. They took us to Harlem Hospital.

"The doctors said something hit my grandfather

on the back of the head. He's in a coma now, and they don't know if he's going to wake up. I wanted to stay with him, but the nurses kept asking if my parents would be stopping by, and eventually I overheard one of them say that she was going to call Child Protective Services to come and pick me up for the night. But my mom and grandfather are the only ones who know I'm here. I couldn't risk being taken away, so I disguised myself in my grandfather's hat and coat, snuck out of the hospital, and ran."

Jin looked concerned. "So you've been wandering the streets of New York by yourself?" She couldn't imagine not having Halmoni and Harabeoji to take care of her. And yet, she suddenly realized, if they hadn't come along, she could've easily been left to fend for herself.

"I've been hiding out in the 135th Street subway station for the past three days," Elvin explained. "Then I saw you guys walking by with your bread. For the record, I never stole anything before that. My mom would kill me if she knew, but I was so hungry . . ."

Alex sprang out of her seat. "Forget the bread, dude! This is awesome! I mean, it's not awesome that your grandfather was hurt, but awesome that we get to help you solve a real-life mystery." She turned to

Jin. "What about this painting that the kid found in the garden?"

"Right. Jarvis Monroe was digging around in the garden and found a potentially rare and valuable painting buried there." Jin flipped a couple pages back in her notebook. "He found it on Tuesday, but they announced the discovery on Wednesday, which was the same night Elvin's grandfather was found in the garden."

Alex paced back and forth, rubbing her temples. "This is strange, very strange." She stopped abruptly in front of Elvin. "Could your grandfather have been doing a little treasure hunting himself that night? Maybe he was searching for more of the paintings, but then something went wrong. And maybe he hit his head in the process, or ran into someone else with the same idea and got into a fight?"

Jin was horrified. "Alex! How could you suggest that?"

"It's not impossible," Alex argued.

Jin glanced at Elvin. "Do you think your grandfather would go searching for buried paintings?"

The truth of the matter was that Elvin didn't know what kind of person his grandfather was or what he was capable of. He didn't think that his mother would send him to live with a man who would risk so much for a painting, but maybe she didn't know her own father that well, either.

"I'm not sure. I guess it's possible," Elvin answered quietly.

Alex softened her gaze. "Do you have anything of your grandfather's that might help us figure out what's going on?"

"Just the goat. And this." Elvin fished a crumpled note card out of one of his grandfather's coat pockets and slid it across the table to Alex, who scanned it and then passed it to Jin. At the top of the card, printed in raised black font, were the letters SMH. The note itself was handwritten in neat cursive.

J—

Please let bygones be bygones. I need to speak with you at once. Call me as soon as you can.

Yours Sincerely,
VMS

"This doesn't give us much to go on." Alex started to pace again.

Jin, who had been busy scribbling, looked up from her notebook. "The SMH at the top of the card seems like some kind of letterhead. The thing that I don't get is, if it's SMH's stationery, why would the note be signed VMS? Do you know anyone with those initials?" she asked Elvin, chewing on the end of her pen.

Elvin shook his head.

Jin turned back to her notebook. "Okay, so step one: we need to figure out what 'SMH' and 'VMS' stand for," she said as she wrote. She paused to snap a picture of the note card with her phone, then typed and sent a quick message. "I'm texting this to my friend Rose. She's great at research and should be able to help us to decode the letters. Now for step two . . ." Jin stopped mid-sentence when she heard the slip-slap sound of Halmoni's sandals approaching. She put her finger up to her lips and whispered, "Don't say anything." Alex and Elvin nodded as Halmoni emerged from behind a stack of boxes.

"Why so quiet? What's going on?" Halmoni demanded.

"Nothing, Halmoni." Jin smiled. "Thank you for the food. It was very good."

"Yes, very good. Thank you," Alex echoed.

"I loved the kimchi. Thank you very much," Elvin added.

"You welcome very much." Halmoni beamed. A

split second later, she was kicking everybody out. "Okay, Jinnie, it's late. Time for your friends go home now."

"Let's meet tomorrow morning," Alex said once Halmoni had gone back to the front of the store.

"But where is Elvin going to stay tonight? We can't send him back out into the streets. Maybe there's some kind of place for homeless, er . . . I mean, kids who are on their own." Jin punched in a search on her phone.

"Wait a second, I have an idea. Someone give me a pen," Alex said, whipping a monograph notepad out of a bag in her cart. Jin passed her a pen, and Alex quickly scribbled something on two sheets of the pad, then neatly tore them off and folded the notes. "Let's go," she said.

"Hey, you!" Halmoni pointed at Elvin before they could slip out of the store.

"Take this. Might get hungry later." She handed him a bag of groceries and a jar of her prized kimchi. Maybe Halmoni actually did have a soft spot somewhere in her fussy heart, Jin thought, proudly.

But as Jin followed Alex and Elvin to the door, Halmoni frowned. "Jin, where you go? Too late to be out."

"Can I just walk them home? I won't be more than an hour, promise," Jin pleaded.

"Not today." Halmoni crossed her arms. Jin knew her answer was final.

"Sorry, guys, I can't come."

"Okay. I'll meet you here tomorrow, and then we'll hook up with Elvin," Alex whispered. Jin gave her a quick thumbs-up as Halmoni picked up her broom again and, jabbing at their feet, swept the two of them out the door.

CHAPTER 7

Elvin lagged several paces behind Alex once they left the bodega. Even pulling a shopping cart, she walked so fast he could barely keep up. She also hadn't bothered to tell him anything about where they were going. He didn't quite know what to make of this girl, who seemed as demanding and unpredictable as the city itself.

After several more blocks, Alex stopped in front of a modern, expensive-looking apartment building and was about to go inside when Elvin grasped her coat sleeve to stop her.

"Wait! I can't go in there. They'll just kick me out." He hunched his shoulders, shrinking even further into his massive coat.

"Don't worry, my dad works for the company that owns this building. I've got everything under control." She yanked open the tall glass doors.

Inside, Elvin hung back near the entrance, swiveling his neck to take in the pristine lobby, with its gleaming white stone tiles and ultra-modern fountain.

Alex parked her cart beside him and marched straight to the reception desk.

"Hola, José," she called. A man dressed in an elegant suit stood up from behind the desk to shake Alex's hand.

"Hola, Miss Roebuck. How can I help you today?"

"I'm here to drop off our latest celebrity guest. He goes by E," she said, gesturing toward Elvin with an exaggerated, exasperated sigh, then leaned in closer to José and lowered her voice. "Apparently, he's a big star on one of those silly kid shows, and he's in town recording his first record at Sony—as if anyone really wants to hear him sing or rap or whatever he does. Anyway, the studio asked my dad to put him up in 6H so that he can focus on writing songs and so they can keep him away from the press until the official launch. You know the drill. We just need the key."

Frantically, José began to riffle through stacks of paper on his desk, a confused look on his face. "I, uh, don't see any 'E' on our VIP guest list. And there's no rental agreement from Sony on file."

Alex didn't flinch. "There is no agreement. Dad is doing this as a favor to one of his friends over at Sony. Didn't his secretary call?" Alex asked calmly. José shook his head.

"Dad was afraid this might happen. He has a new

secretary, Brenda, and she must've forgotten. She's really busy with that big new project. He gave me a note to give to you. Just in case. There's also a note from E's parents saying it's okay for him to stay here by himself." Alex handed him the notes that she'd written back at the bodega.

José glanced at Elvin skeptically. "How old is he?"

Alex didn't blink. "Sixteen, but he's *really* short for his age."

"Are you sure about this? Maybe I should call your dad."

Alex shrugged. "You can, but he's in one of his moods. He just threatened to fire the entire front desk staff at another building for not watering the lobby plants. I hate to think what would happen if he finds out that you kicked America's next Justin Bieber out onto the cold, cruel streets of New York City."

José's face turned red as he handed her a keycard.

"Thanks, José." Alex grinned sweetly, and gestured for Elvin to follow her.

"Sixteen?" Elvin fumed once they were in the elevator. "Sixteen? Look at me! I can barely pass for nine. How are we going to get away with this?"

"*Hello*, we just did." Alex waved the keycard at him. "People will pretty much believe anything if you tell them a good enough story and it's in their best interest to go along with it," she said as the elevator doors slid open.

Alex led the way to 6H. She unlocked the door and flicked on a light to reveal a medium-sized studio apartment. The first thing Elvin noticed was the wall of windows at the front of the apartment, and the expanse of sky and buildings, which seemed so close, it felt like they were part of the living room. Then he saw the rest of the apartment, which was bursting with furniture.

"Be careful, it's kind of cluttered in here," Alex warned. Elvin counted three sofas, two overstuffed armchairs, four coffee tables, along with several rolled-up carpets, paintings, sculptures, and coatracks scattered around the room.

"This unit is where all the furniture from the model apartments comes to die once the apartment gets rented," Alex explained. Elvin cringed. He wished she hadn't used that word, *die*. With his mom, and now his grandfather in the hospital, death was creeping a little too close for comfort. But Alex didn't notice his uneasiness. She was already scaling sofas and chairs.

"I think one of these sofas pulls out into a bed. Found it!" She pounced on a green couch that was nearly buried under piles of cushions and started flinging the extra pillows across the room. Elvin climbed over furniture mountains to help.

"So is your family rich, or what?" Elvin asked as they worked.

"First of all, that's a rude question. And why would you think my family was rich?"

Elvin gestured around the room. "This building? All this expensive furniture?"

"I told you, my dad works for the owners of the building, so we get a few perks. Now, I have a question for you. What do you think of New York so far?"

"It's cold. And very dirty."

Alex laughed. "That's true. Most people only see the trash on the streets and the dirt on the buildings. But beneath the grimy surfaces, everything has a story. You just have to take the time to look for the truth."

For a second, Elvin didn't know if she was talking about the city or herself. Either way, he felt like both were hiding something from him. Even though he'd just met her, he already felt like Alex was keeping her own story a well-guarded secret beneath that ripped-up jacket of hers. And New York? As far as he could tell, the city was one big stinking pile of confusion, loneliness, and danger . . . and he'd just stepped right in the middle of it. The sooner he got out of here, the better.

"Kitchen is over here. Phone and computer are over there. You can use the Wi-Fi, but try not to make too many phone calls—we don't want to attract any attention. Towels and stuff are by the bathroom." Alex pointed around the room. "Oh, and you need some clothes." Alex whipped out her phone and dialed a number. "What size are you, small?"

Elvin nodded, embarrassed, while Alex instructed whoever was on the other end of the phone to deliver a few pairs of shoes, pants, shirts, and a jacket to the apartment. She rattled off a credit card number from memory and hung up. "I'll tell José to leave the package outside of the apartment door when the clothes arrive; that way you won't even have to go downstairs to pick it up."

"Um, thanks for the clothes and all, but are you sure it's okay if I stay here?" Elvin asked. "What if someone comes up here?"

"No one will come. José won't say anything to my dad, and I'll tell him that the apartment is off-limits to the staff. So just keep a low profile."

"If you say so." Elvin was not a hundred percent convinced, but it was either stay here or spend another night in the subway station.

"Here's my number. Jin and I will be back tomorrow." Alex handed him a slip of paper and was gone.

As soon as the door closed behind her, Elvin made his way to the computer to look up the number for his mom's hospital in California. She was the one person in the world that he needed to talk to right now. He plopped down on the nearest couch and dialed, holding his breath while the nurse looked up his mom's name and bracing himself for bad news. Thankfully, the nurse just transferred him, and after two rings, his mom answered.

"Mom!" he said, happy to hear her voice.

"Elvin? Thank goodness! I was starting to worry." Her voice sounded faint and far away. "Honey, how are you?" she asked. "I hadn't heard from you, and nobody answered when I called your grandfather's apartment. Have you two been busy?"

"Yes, real busy." Elvin pinched himself to keep from crying. "I've been seeing a lot of the city." He tried to sound cheerful. "How are you?"

"Oh, so-so. I got approved for a new experimental treatment that the doctors are really excited about."

"That's great, Mom!"

"It'll probably mean me staying in here and you staying in New York a while longer."

Elvin's heart buckled. "That's okay. I just want

you to get better," he said, unable to hide the disappointment in his voice.

"I know this is not what either of us wants, but let's shift the perspective and look at this situation another way," his mom said.

A small smile crept across Elvin's face. Whenever he had a problem, his mom always encouraged him to try and see it from different angles in order to find the best solution.

"Think about it," his mom continued. "I get the opportunity to try out a promising new treatment, and you have the chance to experience one of the world's greatest cities and get to know your grandfather. That's not such a bad deal, right?"

Elvin nodded. "Right," he said, even though he would've taken going back to California over that deal any day.

"So tell me, how are you getting along with your grandfather? Has he been dragging you out on those nightly walks of his?"

Elvin gulped. "Uh, not exactly." He wished he could tell her what was really going on, but he knew that was impossible. If he even hinted that there was a problem, his mom would drag herself out of her hospital bed and be on the first plane to New York. He didn't want that. He wanted her to get well, so they could both go home. So he decided to distract her from asking too many questions with one of his own. "What's the deal with those walks?" he ventured. "Last week, I asked Grandpa where he went, but he wouldn't tell me anything. Why does he do it? Is he just trying to get some exercise? He acts like he's on some kind of mission."

"It's a long story, sweetie. One which I promise to tell you someday soon." His mom paused to catch her breath. "For now, just know that your grandfather is a complicated man. He was born and raised in Harlem and has devoted much of his life to protecting the neighborhood. His nightly walks are his way of making sure the community is safe for the people who live there. I think he honestly believes that he can prevent bad things from happening. Does that make sense?"

No, it didn't make sense! Nothing did. Elvin wanted to yell, and throw the phone across the room. For once, he wished that someone would just be straight with him. *I can handle it. Please tell me what's going on.* He wished he could say the words out loud, but his mother already had enough to worry about without him adding yet another thing to the list.

"Honey, the nurse is here to give me my meds. I'm going to have to hang up now. Tell your grandfather hello for me. We'll talk again soon, okay?"

"All right." The call disconnected with a soft click before he could say good night. Elvin reached for a nearby cushion and screamed as loud as he could into it. The conversation had left him feeling even more lost and confused than he was before. He tried to sort out the knot of questions tangled in his brain. *What did it mean that his grandfather saw himself as a guardian of Harlem, when, clearly, he had been unable to protect himself? And from what, or whom, did the neighborhood need protecting?* Elvin suddenly got a flash of that night in the garden. *What if whoever had attacked his grandfather had also seen him?*

Elvin stared out into the dark night sky, purple as a bruise. The lights from the buildings across the street looked like hundreds of eyes winking at him. A tremor shivered up his spine. *What if they come for me next?*

Elvin flung open the door when Jin and Alex arrived at the apartment the next morning. "My life is in danger," he said solemnly, peering around the girls to scan the empty hallway. "Quick, get inside. They might be watching."

"Who might be watching?" Alex stomped into the apartment with her loud, heavy boots. "Is it José from the front desk? I explicitly told him that no one was supposed to come up here." She grabbed for her phone to call downstairs.

"No, not José. Them! Out there!" Elvin gestured wildly toward the wall of windows in the living room.

"Your neighbors?" Jin asked, puzzled.

Elvin let out an exasperated sigh. "No, not my neighbors. The people who attacked my grandfather. I started thinking that they could've seen me that night at the garden, and if they did, maybe they're planning to attack me next." Elvin wrung his hands and started to pace.

Suddenly, the shrill sound of a phone ringing echoed through the apartment.

"It's them!" Elvin flung himself to the floor.

Alex burst out laughing. Even Jin couldn't help giggling as she reached for her phone. "It's not *them*," she said. "It's Rose."

"Not funny, guys." Elvin scrambled to his feet.

"It kinda was," Alex quipped.

Jin held up a finger to silence them. "Rose has some information about the note card. Go ahead, Rose," she said, and put the call on speaker.

"Hi, all!" Rose said cheerfully. "I did find out some things. But before I get to that, have you gotten any bites on a new owner for Noodles, Jin?"

"It's only been a day since we put the flyer up, but I'm sure we'll find someone really good."

"I hope so. Noodles can't go to just anyone. He's a very sensitive dog."

"Enough with the dog talk. Can we move on?" Alex huffed.

Jin narrowed her eyes at Alex. "Play nice."

Rose ignored Alex. "Anyway, thank you for your help, *Jin*. Noodles and I appreciate it. Now, about the note card. I think that 'SMH' stands for the Studio Museum in Harlem, whose curator emeritus and board chairwoman happens to be a Dr. Verta Mae Sneed, or, 'VMS.' I sent you a link where you can learn more about the museum."

"This is awesome! Thanks, Rose," Jin said.

"You're welcome, *Jin*," Rose said pointedly, and clicked off.

"We should look up the link . . ." Jin started.

"Got it!" Alex held up her phone. She read aloud. "Located on historic 125th Street, the Studio Museum in Harlem was founded in 1968 by a group of African American artists and community members to exhibit and promote the work of artists of African descent from Harlem and beyond. In addition to collecting and exhibiting the work of renowned historical masters such as Romare Bearden, Jacob Lawrence, and Elizabeth Catlett, the museum is also committed to nurturing and promoting the careers of emerging artists through its artist-in-residence program." Alex looked up. "The museum is only a few blocks away, and it's open today." She made a beeline toward the door. "Field trip, anyone?"

Even on a Sunday, the streets of Harlem were practically vibrating with the noises, smells, and energy of hundreds of bodies jostling for precious space. On either edge of the sidewalk, vendors hawked their wares, their flimsy tables sagging beneath the weight of books, incense, jewelry, and clothing. Churchgoers wove their way around late-night partiers straggling home, and everyone stepped over and generally ignored the sick and the homeless people slumped in doorways, or, in one case, stretched out in the middle of the sidewalk. People's lives were happening all around. They intersected, sometimes even crashed into one another, but still somehow managed to remain separate.

It's easy to be invisible here, Elvin thought as the sweet and bitter smell of burnt sugar mingled with the salty, greasy scent of charred meat flooded his nostrils. They were passing by a row of carts selling roasted nuts and kebabs.

Alex nudged him. "We call that street meat," she said, and pointed to a cart. "Nobody really knows what it is. You'll probably want to avoid it." She winked.

"Thanks for the tip," Elvin said, even though, to him, the street meat smelled pretty good.

On the corner at the end of the block, a small crowd clustered around a man with a microphone, sweat pouring down his face as he preached. "Greed is a sickness, my friends. It is a hunger that can never be satisfied! It will claim our homes and our livelihoods and turn our community into a tourist attraction. We must treat this evil vice like a monster in our midst!" The man screeched and pointed as the three kids passed. For a split second, Elvin thought that he was pointing at him, but just as quickly, the man shifted his gaze and his finger to someone else. Elvin walked faster to catch up with the girls.

In the middle of the next block, Alex stopped abruptly. "Here we are," she said. Housed in a five-story white building, the Studio Museum in Harlem was easy to miss, even with aqua-green glass around the base of the building and a large metal awning that jutted out over the sidewalk. For Elvin, the most notable thing about the museum's exterior was the American flag waving over the entrance. Instead of the usual red, white, and blue, the stars and stripes were red, black, and green. These colors, Elvin's mom had taught him, symbolized the pride, liberation, and unity of African Americans and African people around the world.

"Let's go in already." Alex pushed through the glass entryway doors, Jin and Elvin right behind her. Inside, the museum was crowded with families and groups of tourists. "Where to now?" Elvin asked.

"Over there," Jin pointed to a large portrait hanging on the wall across from where they were standing. They pushed through the throng of people for a closer look.

"That's Verta Mae Sneed!" she gasped, reading a small placard next to the painting.

From her perch on the wall, Verta Mae peered intently over a pair of impossibly small wire-frame spectacles, balanced near the tip of her long thin nose. Her eyes, cold and dark as onyx, surveyed the room, seeming to capture and follow even the slightest movements of those unfortunate enough to be caught in her stony gaze.

"I don't think she's gonna want to talk to us," Elvin whispered, taking a step back from the portrait.

"Maybe she's not as mean as she looks." Jin cocked her head from one side to the other as she studied the painting. "There could be a really nice person somewhere in there."

"Yes, and maybe I'll be the next Queen of England . . ." Alex chimed.

"Ahem." A woman with a short pageboy haircut and glasses that looked like they came from the same store as Verta Mae's stood grimacing behind them. She wore a headset and held a clipboard in one hand, a walkie-talkie in the other. "May I help you?"

"No thank you. We're just enjoying the *lovely* art," Alex said, her voice dripping with sarcasm.

Jin cleared her throat. "What she means is, we're

doing a school assignment on museum curators, and we'd like to interview Ms. Sneed."

The woman laughed without moving a single muscle in her face.

"I've never seen anyone do that before," Elvin whispered. Alex elbowed him in the ribs.

"Do you have an appointment?" the woman asked.

"Not exactly, but . . ." Jin sputtered.

"Then it's impossible, I'm afraid. *Dr.* Sneed does not give interviews to members of the public. Especially those without an appointment. And besides, Dr. Sneed does not work on Sundays." The woman flipped through a few pages on her clipboard, then frowned in their direction. "However, we do offer free admission to the museum for *students*," she sneered. "Dr. Sneed believes that art has the power to speak directly to people. You might learn something about her simply by viewing the work she's collected here." With that, she spun on her heels, turning her attention to a family of tourists with several small children on the other side of the lobby. "Excuse me, that sculpture is not for climbing!" she barked as she marched toward them.

"I think that woman is a robot," Alex joked.

"This isn't a time for jokes, Alex. What's our plan?" Jin asked as they meandered into the main gallery.

"We find *Dr.* Sneed." Alex shrugged cheerfully.

"But how? You heard Miss Lobby Police. Verta Mae Sneed doesn't give interviews, and besides, she doesn't exactly look like she'd be thrilled to have three random kids come barging into her office, that is, if she's even here." Jin's voice sounded frantic, even to her own ears. How was it possible that she was the only one who was at all worried about this?

"I'll think of something, just give me a minute. In the meantime, take a deep breath and look at the art." Alex grinned.

"Whatever," Jin huffed.

"We should look for a staff directory, or something," Elvin suggested, but neither girl heard him as they wandered off to separate sides of the gallery. His eyes swept the space, carefully scanning each wall of the room's perimeter. And then he saw it, a barely visible line, like a small seam in one of the walls. He walked over to get a closer look and found that the seam was actually an opening for a door. A small placard posted next to it read MUSEUM STAFF ONLY. Elvin glanced over his shoulder before pressing a white button on the door where a knob should have been. There was a soft click as the lock released. Elvin opened the door just wide enough for him to quickly slide through, silent as a whisper.

On the other side of the door, Elvin was engulfed by darkness, thick and heavy as a blanket. He waited for his eyes to adjust, then took a few tentative steps forward, hands stretched out in front of him like a zombie. He hadn't gotten very far when, *whack!* His knee slammed into a sharp corner of a tall desk.

"Ow!" He yelped and dropped to the floor, hugging his knee to his chest. Suddenly, a door in the corridor beyond the desk flew open and Elvin heard a male voice.

"Just a second," the man said, his voice whiny and wheezy, as though just talking was a huge effort. Elvin held his breath and stayed on the floor, praying that the man would go back into his office. He did. "Yeah, I thought I heard something. Can't be too careful around here," he said as the door closed.

Elvin exhaled, then slowly stood up and walked around to the other side of the desk to investigate. Must be a receptionist's station, he surmised as he ran his fingers over the office phone and computer on top of the desk. He also noticed a small stack of papers, and three picture frames in one corner. He picked up one of the frames, and as he tried to make out the smiling faces in the photograph, a soft whirring sound rustled the air behind him. He spun around to see the green eye of a printer, blinking as the machine spit out a piece of paper. Not a second later, a door opened and he heard the voice of the man again.

"No, I don't have it yet. Just gimme a minute, would you? I'm going to get it from the printer now," the man said. "If Sneed has her way, that painting will be hanging in the museum in no time."

Painting? Sneed? Without thinking, Elvin grabbed the document from the printer, stuffed it in his pocket, and ducked under the desk as the man thundered down the hall. He caught a glimpse of the man's squat shadow with its rounded belly and domed head.

"I don't believe this. It didn't print." The man gave the table a kick. "You'd think this museum could afford a decent printer," he wheezed as he waddled back to his office. Elvin scrambled out from under the desk and sprinted back to the gallery to find Alex and Jin.

Five minutes later, Elvin returned to the dark hallway with the two girls.

"Where are we?" Jin whispered.

"I think these are the staff offices. I didn't have a chance to look for Verta Mae's office because there's someone here." Elvin pointed down the hall. "I didn't get a good look at him, but he was in a foul mood. We'll have to be really quiet passing by his door."

"Wait, so what exactly is our goal here?" Jin whispered, her voice trembling slightly as the reality of where they were and what they were about to do sunk in.

"Our goal," Alex sighed impatiently. "Is to find Verta Mae, ask her if she wrote the note, and get her to tell us what it means."

"And if we don't find her?" Jin pressed.

"We check her office for clues and then we leave, okay? Can we get on with it already?" Without waiting for a response, Alex opened the flashlight app on her phone. A puddle of eerie fluorescent white light appeared at their feet. She aimed the light straight ahead, illuminating a corridor lined with doors. "Let's go," she whispered. Jin, though she still had her doubts, followed closely behind.

The three crept down the hallway. Every few feet, Alex pointed her phone light at one of the doors, and they stopped to read the name written there. They tiptoed past the angry man's office, and kept going until they reached the end of the corridor, where there was a set of tall, wooden double doors. Alex aimed her flashlight so that they could read the brass nameplate affixed to one of the doors. It read DR. VERTA MAE SNEED, CURATOR EMERITUS.

"This is it." Alex pressed her ear against a gigantic

door. "I don't hear anything." She reached for one of the knobs and turned. The door was unlocked. Cautiously, they stepped into another dark room. Alex carefully closed the doors and shined her phone light around the space.

But just as they inched forward to take a closer look, the doors flew open behind them and bright light flooded the room.

"What are you doing in my office?" Verta Mae Sneed towered over them. She looked even scarier in person than she did in her portrait, especially now that she was snarling. "You have three seconds to answer me before I have you arrested for trespassing," she hissed.

Jin and Alex were still too frightened to speak, but when he saw Dr. Sneed heading for the telephone, Elvin stepped forward. "We're trying to find out who attacked my grandfather," he blurted out. "We were hoping you could tell us something. I found this the night he was assaulted." Elvin handed her the note he'd discovered in his grandfather's coat pocket.

Verta Mae Sneed gasped. "Your grandfather is Jacob Morrow?" Elvin nodded. "I was so sorry to hear about that unfortunate incident. How's he doing?" she asked, her voice softening.

"He's in the hospital," Elvin said. "And he's

unconscious, so we don't know what happened. If there's anything you can tell us about him—anything that might help us figure out who may have done this and why—I'd really appreciate it."

"Please, have a seat." Verta Mae Sneed positioned herself behind an enormous, dark wooden desk, which seemed to take up most of the room. Jin took out her notebook as she glanced around the office. Books spilled from the tall book cases that lined one side of the room, and almost every inch of available wall space was covered with a piece of art of some sort. On the wall behind her desk hung a large red banner that featured a single green feather.

Interesting, Jin thought, and made a quick sketch of the banner in her notebook as Verta Mae folded her hands on top of the desk and turned to Elvin. "I knew your grandfather many years ago. In fact, we worked together," she began. "Did he ever mention the Invisible 7?"

"No, but I've only known him for three weeks," Elvin explained.

"Well, he may not have told you about it anyway. Those were difficult years. For all of us." She shifted in her chair to glance behind her at the feather on the banner before continuing. "But I digress. The Invisible 7 was a group that your grandfather and I, along with several other young artists and writers, started in the 1960s. Back then, Harlem was a very different community than it is now. There was high unemployment. People were poor and hungry and angry about all the injustice, racism, and discrimination in our city, in our nation. Housing and schools were substandard. The Invisible 7 wanted to change all that. Our mission was to use art and poetry to beautify our neighborhood, to show that everyday people, who are often thought of as invisible, could change their lives and their community." Verta Mae paused, staring past the three of them as though she were watching her memories play out on a screen that only she could see.

"Dr. Sneed? I don't mean to interrupt your story, but in your note you asked my grandfather to call you. What was it that you needed to talk to him about?" Elvin asked.

Verta Mae Sneed snapped back to the present. "Oh, yes, of course. I wanted to ask him about a painting."

A painting? The words sparked a thought in Jin's brain. "Would this have anything to do with the painting that was discovered in the community garden?" she asked.

Verta Mae looked surprised. "I see you've done

your homework. That painting was created by Henriette Drummond, who was a member of the Invisible 7. Henriette was a very talented artist, a prodigy. Her work had begun to attract the attention of galleries and museums around the world, but she stopped painting abruptly early in her career. She and your grandfather were very close, and he was the last person to see Henriette before she left New York and the art world forever."

"So what does this have to do with Elvin's grandfather?" Alex leaned forward in her seat.

"Because her career was so short, Henriette's paintings are extremely rare and, hence, very valuable. Before she disappeared, Henriette claimed to have destroyed all her work, but we always suspected that she wouldn't have gone through with it. The discovery of this latest painting raises the possibility that there may be more out there somewhere," Verta Mae explained. "And if there are more paintings, they would be the jewels in Harlem's crown, and I want to protect them. They mustn't fall into the wrong hands. There are people who care more about what Henriette's paintings would mean for their wallets than what they mean to this community. That is why I wrote to Jacob as soon as I found out about the discovery in the garden. I thought he might know something more about Henriette's work."

Elvin frowned. "So whoever attacked my grand-father may think that he knows where the other paintings are, too. That is, if there are any other paintings."

"It could be," Verta Mae said hesitantly.

"Why did Henriette stop painting in the first place?" Jin asked.

Verta Mae sighed. "I've said too much as it is. You children should stay out of this." Verta Mae stood and walked toward the door, indicating that the meeting was now over. Alex, Jin, and Elvin took her cue and followed.

"The art world may produce works of beauty, but beneath the surface, there is a teeming cesspool of greed—of people who will stop at nothing to get what they want, including harming others," Verta Mae said. "Please call me if anything surfaces about the paintings. Otherwise, for your own safety, please leave this matter to the authorities."

With that, she closed the doors softly behind them, and they were once again in the dark hallway.

"Do you believe that story?" said Alex.

Elvin held up his finger to silence her. "I don't think we should talk here."

"This place is creeping me out, anyway," Alex said. "Let's get out of here."

They started down the hall, so focused on reaching the door that led back to the museum gallery, that they didn't notice a figure lurking in the shadows as they passed. But to be sure, a pair of cold, dark eyes noticed them.

"I know somewhere we can talk," Alex said once they were outside of the museum, and led the way to a small coffee shop around the corner. They slid into a booth, and a waitress promptly appeared with glasses of water. They ordered three hot chocolates and a plate of fries to share.

"That was crazy awesome!" Alex exclaimed once the waitress had left their table.

"It was crazy creepy." Elvin lowered his voice to a whisper. "Especially Verta Mae Sneed."

"Verta Mae Sneed was *totally* creepy!" Alex concurred.

"Yeah, I couldn't figure her out," Jin said. "On the one hand, Dr. Sneed seemed like she was really concerned about Elvin's grandfather, but she was also really interested in Henriette Drummond's paintings."

"She did say that they were valuable, and that she wanted to keep them out of the wrong hands," Elvin added.

"Or maybe she wants them in *her*

hands," Alex remarked as the waitress arrived with their drinks and fries. She squeezed a puddle of ketchup onto her plate, dunked a fry, and stuffed it into her mouth. "Personally," she said, chewing, "I think Verta Mae is after those paintings herself, and all that mumbo jumbo about the dangers and greed of the art world is her way of throwing us off the case."

"Speaking of that, right before we went into the museum, that preacher guy on the corner started talking about the dangers of greed, and how it was like a 'monster in our midst,' I think that's what he said. And then Verta Mae Sneed said almost the exact same thing about greedy people in the art world. Isn't that weird? Everything is so tangled up, it's hard to figure out what is connected to what," Elvin mused.

Jin, who was bent over her notebook, nodded. "You're right, that is a strange coincidence," she said once she'd finished writing. "I just wish we could find out more about Henriette and that painting. Maybe that would help us to figure out why it's so valuable and why anyone else would want it."

"But the authorities haven't released any information about it yet. We don't even know where it is," Alex said.

"What about the kid who found the painting? We could talk to him," Elvin suggested.

"That's a good idea. Jarvis Monroe shouldn't be too hard to get ahold of." Jin whipped out her phone and dashed off a text message to Rose: *Need address for Jarvis Monroe, kid who found $$ art in garden.*

"That reminds me," said Elvin. "When we were at the museum I found—"

"I just thought of something else," Alex interrupted. "Verta Mae asked if your grandfather knew about the paintings. Do you think it's possible that he did?"

Elvin shrugged. "I don't know," he said, and then remembered his last conversation with his mother. "My mom told me that my grandfather has always seen himself as some kind of guardian or protector of Harlem. I know it sounds kind of weird, but I think the walks were his way of patrolling the neighborhood."

"So maybe he knew that there was something that needed protecting in the garden." Alex downed another fry. "We should check out his apartment. Maybe he even has a stash of paintings hidden there," she said excitedly.

"You're forgetting one thing," Elvin said. "I'm locked out. I don't have a key."

Alex shrugged. "So we sneak in."

"Also, the cops may be looking for me."

"So we make sure they don't see us."

"I don't think that's such a good idea, Alex, especially considering how our field trips have gone so far." Jin frowned.

Alex leaned halfway across the table. "Do you two want to find out what happened to Elvin's grandfather or not?" She locked eyes with Elvin, who nodded. "Okay, then we're going to have to take some risks. Who's with me?" She balled her hand into a fist and held it out in front of her. Reluctantly, Elvin touched his fist to hers. The two of them looked at Jin.

"Fine, whatever. But if we get caught, you have to deal with Halmoni." Jin glared at Alex as she added her fist to the circle.

"Good, see you accomplices tomorrow. Just kidding." Alex laughed and threw a ten-dollar bill on the table. Jin's phone dinged as they were getting up to leave.

"Rose just sent me Jarvis's address. It's still early—wanna go see if we can talk to him?"

"Uh, I can't." Alex's eyes shifted. "I've got a thing."

"What kind of thing?" Jin asked eagerly.

"Just a family thing."

Jin looked away. She couldn't help wondering what Alex was hiding.

"I'll go," Elvin chimed in.

"I'm really sorry about bailing on you guys," Alex said as they lingered outside the restaurant. "You two be careful."

"Jarvis Monroe is seven. I doubt he's dangerous," Jin said.

"Just keep an eye on each other," Alex said. "We don't know who might be after that painting." Then she disappeared into the steady flow of people streaming down the sidewalk.

* * *

"I guess this is it," Jin said as she pressed the buzzer for the Monroe apartment. There was no answer. She was about to try again when a group of kids tumbled out the door. "Hey, do any of you know Jarvis Monroe?" she asked.

One little girl, who looked to be about five years old, nodded excitedly. "He's my cousin. But he's not home. He's at the playground," she said, right before another slightly older child clamped a hand over her mouth.

"You're not supposed to tell that kind of stuff to

strangers," the kid warned, and tugged the little girl by the hand as they followed the others, moving in a cluster, like a cloud of children drifting down the street.

The playground was just at the end of the block.

"Which one is he?" Elvin asked when they reached the entrance.

Jin scanned the park. She saw a boy, yelling down to his friends from the top of a slide, who resembled the kid she'd seen on the news. "I think that's him." She pointed. They started toward him. "Hey, Jarvis!" she called when they were close. Jarvis glanced in their direction and then practically dove down the slide. He started running as soon as he hit the ground. Jin and Elvin chased after him.

"Wait!" Jin yelled. Jarvis hesitated, unsure of whether or not to go back. He slowed down just enough for them to catch up with him near a cylindrical tube that looked like an aboveground tunnel. Jarvis clambered inside. Elvin and Jin positioned themselves at either end.

"Jarvis, we don't want to hurt you. We saw you on the news, and we just wanted to ask you a couple questions about the painting you found," Elvin said.

"Did Zig-Zag send you?" Jarvis's voice echoed through the tube.

"No, who's Zig-Zag?" Jin asked.

"Big, mean guy. Pushed me when I wouldn't tell him about the painting," Jarvis said.

"What did he want to know?" Jin leaned over to peek into the tube.

"He wanted to know where the painting was, but I'm not supposed to tell."

"We won't say anything, we promise. Why don't you come and talk to us out here?" Jin coaxed. Jarvis thought about it for a second, then slowly climbed out of the tube.

Jin stuck out her hand to him to shake. "I'm Jin, and this is Elvin."

Jarvis just looked at her. "My teacher says I'm famous, but I'm not giving you my autograph." He grinned.

"That's okay. We just wanted to know what happened to that painting," Jin started.

"I told you, it's a secret!" Jarvis pouted. "I'm not supposed to tell anybody that it's in the hospital." Jarvis's hand flew to his mouth, and his eyes went wide. "Uh-oh." Suddenly, he sprang to his feet and took off. He was halfway across the playground before Jin could even yell, "Stop!"

Alex stood in front of her bedroom mirror. "I am going to be sick. I am literally going to be sick," she muttered to herself, shaking her head with disgust. Dressed in full riding attire, complete with a black velvet hat perched on her head like an enormous black jelly bean, a red jacket with shiny gold buttons that squeezed her waist like an accordion, and pouffy jodhpurs that billowed out around her thighs like sails, she looked like she should be introducing the next act in a three-ring circus.

"Alexandra, are you almost ready?" Alex's mother, Cassandra, waltzed into the room wearing an ensemble identical to her daughter's.

Alex ignored her mother's question. "I don't see why I have to wear this," she groaned.

"You have to wear it because it is the proper apparel for horseback riding, and we are going on an equestrian outing," Cassandra said, joining Alex in front of the mirror. "Besides, the SEEL moms thought it would be so cute if all the parents and kids wore matching outfits." She leaned in close to the glass to apply a coat of reddish-brown lipstick, then smoothed her hair, which was pulled back into an already flawless, shiny black bun. Alex's hair, in contrast, stuck out like a scarecrow's beneath her jelly bean hat. Cassandra frowned at her daughter in the mirror but quickly recovered as her eyes wandered back to her own reflection. "Despite your best efforts to the contrary, we look adorable!" she gushed, and snapped several pictures of the two of them with her phone, Alex scowling in every one.

A few minutes later, Alex and her mom were in the back of her father's Bentley, on their way to the annual Society for Excellence in Education and Leadership equestrian outing in Central Park. Every year it was the same—a bunch of kids and their parents paraded around Central Park on horseback, then sat down to an expensive catered picnic. Alex hated going on these outings. Come to think of it, she even hated this car. When she looked around the neighborhood, she saw tons of ways they could have used the money it cost to do some good. She slouched down in her seat to avoid the curious stares of other drivers and people on the street, who were always peeking into the car, hoping to get a glimpse of somebody famous. *We're not famous!* Alex wanted to shout. *My dad just spent a lot of money on this car.* Why did people think that spending a lot of money on something made it so much more important?

"James, don't forget to stop and pick up the laundry before you come back to the park to get us at four. Also, Mr. Roebuck is coming home from London tonight. His flight gets in at JFK at seven. Please be on time." Cassandra finished running down the day's tasks with James, their family chauffeur. "This is going to be so much fun!" She turned to Alex and squeezed her hand. "When I was growing up, we rode every summer at our house in Sag Harbor. My father kept horses there, you know. It's a shame more young people don't ride horses today."

"Maybe it's because most kids in New York don't have a summer home or their own horses," Alex mumbled.

"Well, you don't have to have a summer home. There are plenty of opportunities to ride horses here in the city, including this ride that SEEL organizes in the park every fall."

"My point exactly," Alex quipped.

"What's that supposed to mean?" Cassandra swiveled in her seat to face her.

"It means that most of the kids in SEEL are rich, too."

"That is simply not true!" Cassandra sputtered. "The Society for Excellence in Education and Leadership is a historic organization that has nourished young people, irrespective of income, and helped them to become upstanding, confident, self-respecting citizens, who make valuable contributions to our society."

Alex crossed her arms. "Whatever. Let's just forget it."

"What is this about, Alexandra?"

Alex took a breath. "I don't have anything against SEEL, it's just that I wish our family could do more of the things that I care about, like volunteering at the local shelters or food pantries. We always have to do these activities like horseback riding, or going to some stupid fashion show or expensive party. None of these things help change the lives of ordinary people."

Cassandra looked as though she'd been slapped. "I'm sorry that you're so dissatisfied with your station in life, Alexandra, and with the exposure and opportunities that your father and I have tried to provide for you."

"It's not that," Alex interrupted before her mother could get going on her speech about how hard her parents worked, how fortunate she was, et cetera, et cetera. "It's just . . . never mind. You don't get it."

"I guess I don't," Cassandra said. They rode in silence the rest of the way. Alex stared out the window, wondering how Jin and Elvin were faring with Jarvis Monroe. She felt bad about not telling them more about her life. But she wanted them to know the real her, not the character she played in her parents' world of make-believe.

At the park, Alex spotted her friend Rad standing away from the SEEL crew, watching a few skater kids at a nearby fountain. It was strange seeing him without his own board—Rad skateboarded everywhere, even in school when the teachers weren't watching. Today the board was nowhere in sight. He was dressed in riding boots and pants, and looked just as ridiculous as Alex felt.

"Nice outfit," Alex said, and fake-punched him on the shoulder.

"You too. Ready?" he asked. Alex nodded, and they both took out their phones and snapped a picture of one another. They'd started taking pictures of each other two years ago, when Rad transferred to Alex's school. Since neither of them wanted anyone at school to know about the corny stuff their parents forced them to do, the pictures were a kind of insurance policy—neither of them could expose the other without being exposed themselves. What happened at SEEL stayed at SEEL.

An idea suddenly occurred to Alex as they walked together back to the stables. "I need your help with something," she said. Rad was really into art, and he also knew a lot about Harlem, since he skated around the neighborhood every day. Maybe he could help them find out more about Henriette Drummond and her paintings. She didn't think Elvin or Jin would mind, so as they rode through the park, she told Rad the whole story about Elvin's grandfather's attack, the discovery of the mysterious painting, and their meeting with Verta Mae Sneed.

Rad listened carefully. A wide grin spread across his face when Alex finished telling her story. "Dude! This is awesome. It's a real-life art mystery. Meet me tomorrow after school in St. Nicholas Park. I think I know just the person who can help."

CHAPTER 10

The next day, Jin decided to skip her after-school activities so that she could get her chores done early at the bodega and meet Alex and Elvin as soon as possible. They had a lot of ground to cover.

Rose cornered her at her locker. "I thought you had your Environment Club meeting on Mondays. Are you heading home?"

"Yeah, Alex, Elvin, and I have some stuff to do today. I think we've got some really interesting leads."

Rose sniffed. "Sounds important, but I hope not so important that you neglect other things."

"Like what?" Jin stopped shoving books into her backpack to look at Rose.

Rose's pale cheeks flushed pink. "Like Noodles. We're running out of time. My mom and I are going to be moving in a few weeks. Has anyone asked about Noodles at the bodega?"

Jin pretended to be busy again with her books as she shook her head, no. It was true that no one had stepped forward to adopt Noodles, but it was also true that Jin had been so busy helping Elvin, she hadn't had time to really look for a new owner for Noodles like she'd promised. "Halmoni told me that customers in the store are always saying how cute he is. And I'll ask around more in the neighborhood. We'll find a home for Noodles soon, I know it."

"I hope so," Rose sighed, which made Jin feel even worse for letting her down.

Jin said good-bye, slammed her locker door shut, and hurried out of the building.

When she got to the bodega, Halmoni made it clear that she was not happy that Jin had missed her club meeting. "Jinnie, you need to put yourself first," she scolded as Jin sped through her chores.

Jin didn't know what to say, or to think for that matter. It was hard feeling pulled in so many directions at once. If her grades suffered, or she missed too many Environment Club meetings, Halmoni would make her cut back on helping her friends. But even though keeping up with her schoolwork and extra-curricular activities was still very important, Jin was also starting to believe that by helping other people you *were* helping yourself. She'd have to find a way to do both, she resolved as she rushed out of the store to meet Alex and Elvin.

As soon as Jin stepped off the elevator on Elvin's floor, Alex rushed down the hall toward her, waving a newspaper above her head like a madwoman. "You are not going to believe this! The Magic Skillet." Alex pointed to an article, buried deep in the Metro section. "It's closed."

"Closed?" Jin reached for the paper.

The Magic Skillet, a veritable Harlem institution, was shut down by health inspectors early yesterday morning due to numerous health code violations, including mice and cockroach infestations. "It doesn't make any sense. We run a clean business. We've never had any violations before. This just came out of nowhere, like the plague of locusts in the Bible," said proprietor Owen Montgomery, whose family has owned and operated the establishment for over fifty years. "We've been noticing the changes in the neighborhood. It's a different clientele. Lots of young people, who like sushi and nitro-foam foods that I can't even pronounce. We believe our

time has passed. We've received an offer to
buy the building, so we've decided to close.

"But we were just there!" Jin looked up from the paper. "I didn't see any mice or roaches."

"I know, it just doesn't add up," Alex sighed, and plopped down on the sofa, tossing the newspaper aside.

Jin sat down beside her and picked up the paper to read through the article again. "Hey, look at this." She pointed to another story on the opposite page. "It says, 'Councilman Markum Reveals Proposed Location of Harlem World Development,'" Jin read aloud. "'Though still awaiting city approval, Councilman Geld Markum has released a map of the proposed location of Harlem World, the Harlem-themed amusement park and entertainment complex, which he hopes will celebrate the rich historic and cultural legacy of the neighborhood—and also boost his bid for reelection.'"

"Let's see." Alex leaned forward. "It's worse than I thought," she groaned, jabbing her finger at the map, which covered a large chunk of the neighborhood. "He's literally trying to take over all of Harlem."

"Maybe it's not so bad. The article does say that

Markum's plan will bring jobs and increased tourism revenue to Harlem. That's got to be good for local businesses," Jin said.

"They always say that, and then local people and small business owners, like the folks at the Magic Skillet, are the ones who suffer the most." Alex walked over to the floor-to-ceiling windows and shook her head sadly as she looked out over Harlem. "This is really bad. But it gives me an idea," she said and whirled around to face Jin. "Harlem World would make a great topic for our neighborhood project for history class. That way we can keep tabs on what Markum is really up to."

"But Ms. Weir said it has to be a project about the past," Jin protested.

"The future is the past. Besides, our assignment, technically, is to pick an aspect of our neighborhood that has shaped its character," Alex argued. "This development is going to completely turn Harlem upside down. If that doesn't count as shaping character, I don't know what does. Are you in?"

"Okay, but you have to talk to Ms. Weir if she gives us any trouble," Jin agreed. "Maybe we can even include the Magic Skillet closing in our project. I mean, what kind of community does Harlem become in the future if places like the Magic Skillet, which are a big part of its past, get totally erased?" she wondered out loud.

"That's exactly what I want to know!" Alex said.

Elvin, who had slipped away to the kitchen, returned with a plate of sliced apples and a jar of peanut butter. "Snacks are served," he said, setting the plate down on the coffee table.

For some reason, Elvin's snack made Alex feel especially moved. Before she bit into it, she held up her apple slice, as if she were proposing a toast. "I would like to say thank you to Elvin for sharing his food. And to restaurants like the Magic Skillet that prepare and donate meals so that everyone in our community can have food to eat. Here's to Elvin and the Magic Skillet."

"To Elvin and the Magic Skillet!" Jin and Elvin repeated. They bit into their apple slices at the same time, then devoured the rest of the slices on the plate, along with almost the entire jar of peanut butter. When they were finished eating, Alex did not waste any time getting down to business.

"So what happened with boy wonder?" she asked.

"Who?" Elvin looked confused.

"The kid who found the painting."

"Oh, him." Jin frowned. "He was a brat, but he did say a couple interesting things." She opened up her notebook to the page where she had written her notes about yesterday's encounter with Jarvis Monroe. "First of all, we found out that we weren't the only ones who'd paid him a visit."

Elvin picked up the story. "Yeah, he said this mean guy named Zig-Zag wanted to know where the authorities had taken the painting after he found it. He pushed Jarvis around a bit when he wouldn't tell him, poor kid."

"But here's the thing," Jin continued. "Jarvis actually did tell us where the painting was. He said that it was in the hospital. What that means, I have no idea."

"Maybe it means exactly what he said. Maybe the painting is actually in a hospital. Not like a patient or anything, but just that they're keeping it there for some reason," Elvin suggested. "I want to visit my grandfather at Harlem Hospital anyway. We could see if anybody's heard anything about the painting while we're there."

Alex nodded in agreement. "I also spoke to my friend Rad yesterday. He said he knows someone who might be able to give us some information about Henriette Drummond, and wants us to meet him in St. Nicholas Park this afternoon," she said.

"And don't forget, we were going to, uh, check out Elvin's grandfather's apartment," Jin said, making a list in her notebook. "Which isn't far from St. Nicholas Park, right? We can meet Rad, and then go to your grandfather's place. That way we kill two birds with one stone."

Elvin cringed as they filed out of the apartment. "Can we please not use words like 'kill'?"

"Sorry, Elvin," said Jin.

"We need to follow up on these leads as quickly as possible if we want to find out who attacked your grandfather," said Alex. "Because whoever is looking for Henriette's paintings is our main suspect. And if those paintings are really as valuable as Dr. Sneed says, we definitely want to get to them first."

St. Nicholas Park looked like a remnant of another era—one before Manhattan had been settled, before the grid of buildings and pavement, streetlights and sewers, structured and organized the island. It was full of sloping rock formations topped by pointy boulders and wild brambles creeping along the ground. It reminded Elvin of the hills that surrounded his house in California.

Alex led them up one of the meandering paths to an area of the park where a bunch of skater kids were hanging out, clustered around park benches and ollie-ing on the stair rails. Alex saw Rad and waved.

"What up, dudes?" Rad skated over, perspiration beading on his forehead. He shook his electric-purple-and-blue dreadlocks, sending droplets of sweat flying everywhere. Jin curled her lip, disgusted, and took a step back. Rad didn't seem to notice. "Man, I almost had that kickflip."

"Yeah, that's a hard one. It took me a while to get it right," Elvin said shyly.

"You skate, dude? Right on!" Rad held up his fist again for Elvin to bump. "You totally need to come skating with us. What kind of board do you have?"

Before Elvin could answer, Alex took over. "I don't mean to interrupt your skater lovefest, but we don't have all day. Rad, were you able to look into that stuff we discussed yesterday?"

Rad slapped his forehead. "My bad, dude. Totally slipped my mind, but hold up a sec. My homey is right over there. He's the one I wanted you to talk to." He dropped his board to the ground and skated over to a group of kids crowded around a park bench. In a few minutes, he returned with an older kid who looked like he had just stepped out of a 1980s break-dancing movie. He wore his hair in a high-top fade and had on a red jacket with black leather patches on the arms and shoulders. A huge gold medallion that said T.J. hung around his neck.

As they got closer, Jin was surprised to see that he was at least sixteen. *What was this kid doing hanging out with a bunch of middle schoolers?* She wondered as the boys reached their circle.

"This is my homeboy, T.J.," Rad introduced the kid. "This dude is an awesome artist. He's like my guru when it comes to graffiti, and all kinds of art, really. He's about to blow up and get his own gallery show, right, T.J.?"

"Yeah, it's definitely in the works. If things go as planned, it won't be long before my name is up in lights." He grinned. Jin rolled her eyes. She already didn't like this guy. Alex didn't seem to like him much, either. She was definitely giving him the evil eye.

"Well, good luck with that," Alex said flatly. "We actually need your help with a little art-related problem," she explained, and then filled him in on the story of Elvin's grandfather's attack and how their search for his attackers had led them to the mysterious painting.

"We were wondering if you knew anything about the painting that was found in a community garden not far from here." Jin turned to T.J. "We think it might be pretty rare."

"I'll ask around, see if there's any word on the street about it," T.J. said. "Did you happen to hear if there were any more paintings like it? What I mean is, artwork like that usually isn't a one-shot deal. There's probably more out there."

"We think there might be more paintings, too. We're going to my grandfather's apartment to see if we can find some clues there," Elvin said.

"Sounds like a plan." T.J. seemed distracted. "Sorry, dudes, don't mean to bail, but there's something I gotta do. I'll look into those paintings for you," he said, and quickly left the park.

"We should go, too," Alex said to Rad. "Thanks for your help, but we've got a lot to do before dark." She raised her eyebrows at Jin and Elvin.

"Oh, right." Jin suddenly felt queasy. She had forgotten about the second half of their mission, the breaking-and-entering part, and she was not looking forward to it.

Alex charged ahead, propelled by the prospect of a new, and possibly dangerous, adventure. Jin walked slower, peering up at the sky, which was overcast and damp, like a sink full of wet rags waiting to be wrung out. She thought about Halmoni, who was probably at this very minute standing at her laundry basin at the back of the store, soaking the day's aprons and towels before dinner. If Jin were there, she'd be hanging up the clean towels on the clothesline that stretched across the storeroom. That was their routine, what they did every afternoon. Jin was only a few blocks from the bodega, but she suddenly felt like she was miles away.

"I'm still not sure this is such a good idea." Elvin fell into step alongside Jin, following her gaze up toward the sky.

"Yeah, I know," Jin said as they slowed down a little more to watch fast moving clouds greedily devouring the meager daylight. Now the sky looked like a heavy balloon threatening to burst and cover the city in thick gray fog.

"What's taking you slowpokes so long?" Alex stopped to wait for Jin and Elvin to catch up. Once they were within reach, she clamped down on each of their arms, dragging them forward.

When they got to 135th and St. Nicholas Avenue, Elvin pointed toward a community garden on the corner. "This is where I found my grandfather. He was right by the entrance here." He shuddered. Alex and Jin took a few tentative steps into the garden.

"That must be where Jarvis Monroe found the painting." Jin pointed to a wooden bench. A series of small holes, where someone had obviously been digging, surrounded it. In fact, as Jin looked around, she noticed there were holes everywhere. "I don't think Jarvis could've done all this on his own. Someone else must've been digging here," she guessed. She reached for her phone to take a picture but realized in her rush to leave she had forgotten it back at the store. She called Alex over and asked her to take a few shots.

"This garden has more craters than the moon," Alex said, aiming her phone at the ground.

"Can we please get out of here? This place gives me the creeps," Elvin called to the girls.

"Coming!" Jin answered as she and Alex trudged back to where Elvin was standing at the entrance. They kept walking.

At 138th Street, Elvin slowed down. "The apartment building is at the end of this block, but the entrance is around the corner. I think one of you should go ahead to make sure we can sneak in without being noticed."

Alex volunteered and ran to the end of the block. She peered around the corner and then ran back. "We've got a problem. There's a squad car with two cops parked across the street from the building. I'm thinking our best bet is to go up the fire escape. I'll show you." They inched closer to the building, and Alex outlined her plan. "We'll have to drop down on all fours when we're passing a window, and each take one landing at a time, but other than that, it should be easy peasy," she explained.

Elvin shook his head. He was starting to get a little frustrated. "I thought the whole point was for us to sneak in. If we go up the fire escape, one of the neighbors, maybe even the police might see us."

"What if I distract the police?" Jin suggested. "I could go over to the car and ask a question while you guys climb up."

"It could work," Alex mused, sizing up the black

metal fire escape snaking along the side of the five-story building. She turned to Jin. "You sure about this?"

Jin gave her a thumbs-up. Alex jumped and yanked down the lowest rung of the fire escape. Once they started up the stairs, Jin took a deep breath, gripped her notebook tightly in her hands, and marched over to the police car. She tapped lightly on the driver's partially open window. The officer, who was just about to bite into a sandwich, sat up abruptly and nearly dropped his food.

"Sorry," Jin said, and took a step back.

"Something we can help you with?" the officer grumbled, annoyed to have his meal interrupted.

"Um, I live over there." Jin gestured vaguely behind her. "I just happened to see you two officers out here, and I was wondering if you could help me with my homework."

The driver looked over at his partner. "Eh, Ricky, she wants us to help her with her homework." He chuckled.

"Not if she wants to pass, she don't." Ricky nudged the driver and the two burst out laughing.

"What is it you need help with?" the first officer asked.

Jin quickly came up with a standard, garden-variety career question. "We're supposed to interview people from different professions to find out more about what they do. For example, what is the day in the life of a police officer like?"

The officer leaned back in his seat, the vinyl covering squeaking beneath him. "That all depends. Most days it's breaking up fights, responding to burglary calls, you know, your run-of-the-mill criminal activity. Some kid gets his bike stolen, or somebody's car or house gets broken into, stuff like that. Every now and again, we get to chase somebody. Remember that guy last week, Rick? The one running off with the TV? Tackled him before he got two blocks."

"Interesting." Jin tried hard not to roll her eyes as she pretended to take notes.

"Sometimes, though, a special assignment comes up, like now." The officer motioned her closer to the window. "You didn't hear it from me, but we're on a stakeout, looking for a missing kid. Higher-ups are really interested in this kid for some reason. Got strict instructions on this one to bring him in."

Jin scribbled quickly and glanced over her shoulder just in time to see Elvin's feet sliding through a top-floor window. Alex was nowhere in sight. *She must already be inside,* Jin thought as she slammed her notebook shut. "That's all I need. Thanks officers," she said, scurrying away.

"Hey, kid, stop for a sec. We want to ask *you* a couple questions," one of the officers called from the car. Jin pretended not to hear and kept walking. When she heard the creak of a car door opening, she broke into a run. She lept up the front steps of Elvin's grandfather's apartment building and swung open the heavy entryway door. She slammed her palms against the two rows of buzzers, ringing several at a time. Someone buzzed her in just as the police officers reached the front stoop. Jin slid through the second door and pushed it shut behind her, then ran up the stairs to the fifth floor, where Alex and Elvin were waiting in the hallway.

"They're looking for you," Jin told Elvin once she'd caught her breath. "The cops said that they have orders from high up to find a missing kid. I think they wanted to ask me some questions about you, but I got away."

"Great. Now I'm officially a wanted man," Elvin sighed.

"It'll be okay." Jin patted his arm.

"Can we just do what we came here to do, before we all end up in jail?" Alex pushed past the two of them back into the apartment. Jin and Elvin followed her into the pitch-black living room. Within seconds, they heard a loud thud and metallic clank.

"Yeow!" Alex groaned. "I just crashed into something. I think I killed my shins."

"Could you please not use that word?" Elvin grumbled. A small sliver of light peeked into the room as Alex inched back the curtain of one of the windows overlooking the street. "The cops. They're gone. Maybe they went for backup," she whispered. "Let's hurry up and look around so we can get out of here before they come back." Alex flicked on her phone's flashlight and shined it around the living room, which was overflowing with books. "How are we ever going to find anything here?"

"Why don't we start in a less crowded room," Jin suggested, and Elvin led them into the tiny kitchen. After a quick look around, they moved on to the bedroom.

"Light's not coming on." Elvin flicked the switch on and off.

"With your grandfather in the hospital, maybe the electricity got turned off," Jin suggested.

Elvin was glad it was dark so that the girls couldn't see him blush. "My grandfather paid the bill, if that's what you're getting at," he said.

"I didn't mean that he didn't pay, I just . . . never mind," Jin said, flustered.

"Let's just look around. Jin, you take the bed and nightstand. Elvin, you take the dresser. I'll take the closet," Alex directed as she placed the cell phone with the flashlight shining on the nightstand. The light fell on Elvin's cell phone and keys, which he'd left behind the night of the attack. He put them in his coat pocket before heading over to the dresser.

Jin riffled through the nightstand drawer and poked her head under the bed. She didn't find anything, so she meandered over to the dresser to help Elvin inspect the drawers.

"So are you and your grandfather close?" she asked as they searched through rolled-up pairs of socks and neatly folded shirts. Elvin shook his head.

"To be honest, I never knew he existed before my mom got sick. She left home and moved out to Cali when she was seventeen. I guess she must have cut things off with my grandfather because, up until now, I didn't think we had any other family. But I guess I was wrong. She knew about him, she just never bothered to tell me," Elvin said with a little sharpness in his voice. He and his mom had always told each other everything. How could she have kept such a big secret from him? He felt a small lump of sadness mixed with anger rising in his throat. But now was not the time to think about that, so he swallowed hard to keep it down.

Jin sighed. "I never knew my mom, either. But neither did my grandparents, or at least that's what they told me. My mother left me at their church in Queens. Halmoni said she knew I belonged to her before she even saw me."

"Aren't you ever curious about your mom?" Elvin asked.

Jin considered the question for a minute. The fact that she didn't know her mother was simply that, another fact. Her mother leaving her was like the breath that singers take at the beginning of a song. Just a thing that happened before her real life began. She shrugged. "I keep these notebooks where I record the stuff that I observe every day. Maybe one day I'll get a clue about her, but I don't really think that much about it. "

"Hey, guys, a little help!" Alex called. Jin and Elvin ran over to the closet. "There's a box back there," Alex pointed. "I need help reaching it." Jin and Elvin dove into the packed closet, kicking aside shoes and pushing coats and suits out of the way to make a path for Alex to climb through. She got on all fours and crawled to the back of the closet, grabbed a shiny black box and crawled back out.

"What's in it?" Jin asked. Alex lifted the lid. Inside was a woman's hat, shaped like a half sphere, with a small bouquet of feathers sewn onto one of the sides. A plain white business card rested on top of the hat. Alex grabbed it and held it up to her phone light. "'Compliments of I. Drummond,'" she read.

"Drummond? That's Henriette's last name!" Elvin remarked. But before they could examine their find more closely, they heard a scraping noise coming from the living room.

"What's that?" Elvin asked.

"I don't know. Sounds like it's coming from the front of the apartment. Let's go back into the kitchen. We can check out the living room from there," Alex suggested. "In the meantime, this is coming with us." She slammed the lid back on the hatbox and tucked it underneath her arm, then grabbed her cell phone and led the way into the kitchen, just as a small pool of light from the outside hall fell across the living room floor.

"Someone's here!" Jin started to panic. Elvin and Alex put their fingers up to their lips to quiet her.

"These old apartments always smell like cabbage," a whiny male voice said from the now open front door. "And they're so tiny. How do roaches even live in these boxes?" The voice moved closer. "It feels different in here tonight. Does it feel different to you?"

"No, it don't feel different. Why should it?" a second, gruffer male voice asked.

"And what about the lights?" Whiny Voice demanded.

"You told me to cut the electricity, remember?"

"Why would I tell you to do something so stupid? We have to go through this place top to bottom, and we can't see anything. How are we going to find a bunch of paintings in all this junk? Did you at least remember to bring the flashlights?" The man angrily swept a stack of books from the coffee table.

"Yeah, got 'em right here in the bag."

"Did you hear that? Paintings!" Alex whispered.

"Yes, but we've got to get out of here before they find those flashlights. Let's go back to the window." Jin pointed and they tiptoed in the direction of the bedroom.

"You guys go first. I'll keep watch," Elvin said.

"Call the police," Jin whispered.

"Can't. My phone is dead. It hasn't been charged for a week."

"Mine just died, too," Alex added. "Let's just get out of here."

Carrying the hatbox, Alex carefully slid out of the window onto the fire escape. Jin followed. Elvin was about to climb out the window when he remembered that he'd left his phone charger in the nightstand drawer. He made his way over to the nightstand and grabbed the charger. As he headed back to the window, his foot tugged the cord of the nightstand lamp, sending it crashing to the floor.

"What was that?" shouted one of the men from the kitchen. They ran to the bedroom. Elvin dove for the window, but he was too slow. He only managed to get half of his body out before the men grabbed his legs. He gripped the windowsill, kicking wildly. His foot made contact with one of the men's faces. The guy reeled backward, releasing Elvin to grab his own nose. It gave Elvin just the leverage he needed to wriggle out of the other man's grasp and onto the fire escape landing, scraping his cheek on a nail sticking out of the window frame in the process. He felt his skin opening, like a zipper coming apart. Cool blood oozed down his cheek, which began to sting once the chilly fall air hit the open wound, but he didn't stop moving.

Elvin scrambled to his feet and flew down the fire escape's narrow metal stairs. He jumped off the bottom step and kept running, until his toe caught on something on the sidewalk and, suddenly, he was facedown, staring at a patch of broken concrete. He thought he heard someone calling him, but he couldn't answer. Instead, he curled up in the cloud of dark fog that was settling over him, and let it carry him, far, far away.

As Elvin's eyes fluttered open, the kindly face of an old man staring down at him slowly came into focus. The man had a white beard and bushy white eyebrows that stood out against his sandy skin. When he smiled, as he did now, his eyebrows rose then fell in one fluid motion. Elvin imagined they were waving at him.

"Welcome," the man spoke in a hushed tone. "You've been gone for a little while."

"Elvin, this is Dr. Whitmore. He's the doctor at the shelter where I volunteer, so you're in good hands." Elvin heard Alex's voice behind him, but when he tried to sit up to look at her, his head started spinning and he felt a searing pain on the right side of his face.

"Take it easy, young man," said Dr. Whitmore. He placed a hand on Elvin's shoulder, easing him back onto the pillows of an antique sofa where he had been resting. The doctor shined a small light into his eyes and made him follow his finger up and down, right to left. "I don't think you have a concussion, but you did bang yourself up pretty badly, so you have to be careful. No strenuous activities for a while," he instructed Elvin.

"Wait a minute, what happened? Where are we?" Elvin tried to sit up again.

"Didn't you hear the doc? You need to rest," Alex admonished as she and Jin sat down next to him on the couch.

"Okay, I'm resting. Now tell me. Everything," Elvin demanded. The girls exchanged glances before Jin started to speak.

"When we got out of the building, we realized that you weren't behind us and thought that something must be wrong. The police we saw earlier hadn't come back—not that I would've gone to them anyway, so I ran to the corner store to get help, and Alex kept a lookout for you at the building. I told the store owner that someone had broken into your apartment and that you were still up there. He sent several of his sons rushing over to the building with baseball bats. Then you came running from the fire escape and slipped on some uneven pavement."

Elvin frowned. He couldn't help but feel a little bit cheated. He had fought off and escaped two dangerous thugs, only to be taken down by . . . the sidewalk? It didn't seem fair.

"Did the guys from the store catch the men who broke into the apartment?"

"Unfortunately, no. The burglars must have heard them coming. We didn't get a look at them, and we left before the police arrived," Jin explained.

"What about my face?" Elvin touched his bandaged cheek and then he remembered. "I think I cut myself on a nail as I was going through the window."

"I knew we couldn't go to a hospital, since everyone seems to be looking for you, so I figured Dr. Whitmore was the next best thing. Even though, technically, he's retired, he still knows his stuff." Alex gestured toward the doctor.

Dr. Whitmore grinned and extended his hand. "I'm happy to be of service, and pleased to make your acquaintance, Elvin."

"Yours too, sir. Thank you for helping me."

"Now, if I may be so forward as to inquire, what's this about people looking for you? Am I harboring a wanted man?" Dr. Whitmore asked, raising his bushy brows. Elvin squirmed.

"It's complicated," he said hesitantly.

Alex elbowed him gently. "We can trust Dr. Whitmore." Jin nodded in agreement, and the three of them told him the entire story, from Elvin's grandfather's attack to the encounter with the burglars at his apartment.

When they finished, Dr. Whitmore studied Elvin for a moment. "Your grandfather is Jacob Morrow."

"Yes!" Elvin exclaimed, eyes widening. "Do you know him? Does *everybody* in Harlem know my grandfather?"

"It is indeed a small and bizarre world we live in. Your grandfather and I were very good friends back in medical school. I was so sorry to read about the attack. I've been meaning to go look in on him, but these old bones aren't what they used to be. I don't get out much, except to go to the shelter. I hope he is recovering well."

"I haven't been able to see him," Elvin said sadly.

"You will, son." Dr. Whitmore squeezed his shoulder. "Did you know that your grandfather was at one time planning to become a doctor?" He asked. Elvin shook his head.

"Well, he was, but his heart wasn't really in it. You see, I come from a long line of physicians, so my fate was pretty much sealed. I had no choice but to become a doctor, but your grandfather was always more of an artist. Literature was his passion. He wanted to be a writer. He even founded an informal organization for those of us med students starving for a creative outlet. It was called the Union of Art and Medicine.

"We'd sit at the kitchen table in his tiny apartment and talk about books, art, and music. It was a wonderful time. And this is what he'd always say to open up our meetings." Dr. Whitmore stood and in a bellowing voice proclaimed, " 'Let our thoughts march unfettered around this table, as in the world. We allow no man to imprison our minds and hearts.' "

"That sounds really awesome. I think I would like school more if I had a club like that." Alex grinned.

"So what happened after that?" Elvin leaned forward.

"Your grandfather eventually dropped out of medical school, and we lost touch. I heard that he'd gotten involved in some sort of community arts organization. Several years passed without seeing one another, and then, one day, he showed up at my office."

Jin scooted to the edge of her seat. "What did he want?"

"He wanted to speak to me in regards to a young woman with whom we were both acquainted. And also to give me something he felt was of great importance."

"What did he give you?" Alex asked.

Dr. Whitmore paused. "Before I answer that, I'm

afraid I have to tell you another long story. Will you indulge me?" Alex, Jin, and Elvin nodded enthusiastically, and he continued.

"Back in the late 1960s, when I was young physician doing my residency at Harlem Hospital, I'd often take a stroll around the hospital to keep myself awake when I was on call nights. One evening, I encountered this striking young woman in the hospital lobby. Her hair was braided in two pigtails and she was wearing— what do you call them?—coveralls, that's it, like a painter. But the most peculiar thing was that she was perched on top of a tall ladder, staring at a large blank wall. I asked her if she needed help, and she responded, 'No, why do you ask?'—as if it were the most normal thing to find oneself sitting atop a ladder in a hospital lobby. I was struggling to extract my proverbial foot from my mouth when she started laughing, and I knew she'd been teasing me. Then she said, and this I remember clearly, 'I was just envisioning.'

"I later learned that she was a young artist who'd been hired to paint a mural in the lobby. From that day on, I made it my business to stroll by to observe her progress. She always looked hungry—and I'd often offer to split my lunch with her. She never said much, which was fine by me. I just enjoyed watching her work; the thrill of seeing people and objects emerge on the wall! The piece was a vibrant series of scenes from everyday life in Harlem: children playing, people doing their shopping, neighbors chatting, that sort of thing." Dr. Whitmore smiled at the memory, and then frowned.

"She told me that she'd been commissioned to paint a second mural in the hospital, and seemed pretty excited about it. But just as she was nearing completion of the first, her disposition changed dramatically. She became withdrawn, sad. When I'd ask her what was wrong, she'd simply say, 'I've made so many mistakes. I've ruined everything.' I thought that she was talking about her painting, so I told her again and again how wonderful it was, but nothing seemed to cheer her up.

"The last time I saw her was the night she finished the painting. I was there to witness the last brushstroke. However, instead of celebrating her accomplishment, the young woman calmly climbed down from her ladder and proceeded to rip up all the lovely sketches and miniature paintings that she'd made in preparation for the mural. I was so busy admiring the final piece, that I didn't realize what she had done until it was too late.

" 'Why?' I asked. 'Why ruin your beautiful work?'

She just shook her head. 'No more beauty. I'm finished. It's over,' she said and left the hospital. I never saw her again."

"That's sad," Jin said.

"What does this have to do with my grandfather?" Elvin asked.

"Well, about a month after the young woman disappeared, Jacob came to my office. It turns out that he and the painter were friends and also members of the same artist collective. She had told Jacob of our acquaintance and asked him to give me her regards. He wouldn't tell me why she'd left, only that she was fine. And he gave me this." Dr. Whitmore stood up slowly, hobbled over to a desk on the other side of the room, and took a manila envelope out of the top drawer. "He told me to keep it somewhere safe, even if I never read it. To be honest, I never knew why Jacob would give me this. Back in med school, your grandfather had a reputation for foisting obscure books on his friends, as if we didn't have enough to read already. I thought it odd that, after all those years, he would show up at my door with a book. In any case, I feel like you are its rightful owner," he said, and held the envelope out to Elvin.

Elvin opened it and slid out a thin paperback

book, with a plain white cover that read *The Life of the Invisibles* in black block print. "It's a book of poems," he said, flipping through it.

"The Invisibles. Wasn't that the name of the artist group Elvin's grandfather was in with Verta Mae Sneed?" Alex asked.

"Oh, yeah, right. It was the Invisible 7," Jin recalled, and turned to Dr. Whitmore. "Do you happen to remember the name of the young woman, the artist?"

"Henriette something-or-other. I don't remember the last name." Dr. Whitmore scratched his head.

"Could it be Drummond?" Alex asked.

Dr. Whitmore smiled and nodded. "That's right! Henriette Drummond!"

"That's the artist whose painting we're looking for. This is getting really bizarre." Alex glanced at Elvin and Jin.

"The hospital!" Jin stood up suddenly. "Maybe that's what Jarvis Monroe was talking about. I think you were right, Elvin. The painting may be at the hospital."

Elvin sat up. "We have to get to the hospital."

"Whoa, cowboy, even I have to nix that idea," Alex said. "First of all, we were nearly killed. Second of all, you still need to rest. And third of all, the owner of the store near your grandfather's apartment called the cops, remember? By now, they've probably got an officer posted at your grandfather's hospital room. In a couple of days, maybe, but not tonight."

"I agree with Alex, and besides, I have to get home. It's way past my curfew," Jin said.

"We should all be going," Alex got up. "Is he okay to travel?"

"He should be fine. I would just watch him overnight, and if he has any issues, bring him by. In any case, call me tomorrow to let me know how he's doing," Dr. Whitmore instructed.

"Thanks again, Doc," Elvin said as they headed out the door.

Outside, they huddled against the cold for a moment in the building's entryway.

"So what's the plan?" Jin asked.

"Clearly, we've got a lot to process. But for tonight, I'm going to stay at the apartment with Elvin, since Dr. Whitmore said someone should watch him. I'll just tell my parents I'm sleeping at a friend's house," Alex said. Jin felt a slight twinge of envy. Why couldn't Halmoni let her have more freedom like Alex's parents?

"Do you think you could bring the hat with you to school tomorrow?" Jin asked. "I'd like to show it to my friend Rose. She knows everything about fashion, and she might be able to tell us something about it."

"That's a great idea, Jin," Elvin said.

"Yes, it is. I'll definitely bring it, unless you want to take it now." Alex held the box out to her. Jin shook her head.

"I know Halmoni's waiting up for me, and she's going to ask me a million questions if I come in with it."

"Then it's settled." Alex raised her arm to hail a passing black livery car. The car swerved sharply and came to a stop right in front of them. The three got in and were whisked away into the night.

* * *

Just as she suspected, Halmoni was waiting at the front door in her bathrobe when Jin got home. But before she could start yelling, Jin rushed over and tightly wrapped her arms around her. She hadn't planned to do it, but seeing her tiny grandmother standing in the doorway of their tiny apartment, sent a wave of relief through her entire body. Halmoni hugged her until her body went limp and she was nearly asleep on her feet. With all that had happened that night, Jin realized how happy—and lucky—she was to be back home.

Halmoni waited until Jin had changed into her pajamas and climbed under the covers, then she sat down on the edge of her grandaughter's bed with her arms folded. "What's going on with you, Jin? You in trouble?" She frowned.

"No, not exactly," Jin sighed, barely awake. Halmoni, clearly not willing to leave it at that, did not budge. Jin rubbed her eyes and forced herself to sit upright. Leaving out huge chunks of the story— namely the parts about the mysterious painting, breaking into the building, and being chased by dangerous thugs—she told Halmoni about how she and Alex had been helping Elvin to find out what had happened to his grandfather, and how they had taken him to see Dr. Whitmore after he had tripped and hurt himself earlier that night.

"We have to help this poor boy," Halmoni said quietly, lost in thought.

"Are you . . . okay, Halmoni?" Jin ventured. Halmoni absentmindedly patted her leg.

"You go to sleep now, Jinnie."

"So I'm not grounded?" Jin knew it was a risk asking. After all, she didn't want to remind Halmoni to ground her if, by chance, she'd forgotten.

Halmoni shook her head. "Not yet, but still possi-bility. You must be careful, Jin. You come to me and Harabeoji if you need help, understand?" Halmoni said firmly.

Jin nodded. But she knew she would eventually have to disobey Halmoni in order to track down Jacob Morrow's attacker. She hated lying to her grandmother, but sometimes rules had to be broken for the greater good.

The next morning before school, Jin headed down to the bodega earlier than usual. She swung open the door, and then a thought made her stop abruptly. *Halmoni*. Her grandmother had left the apartment for the store long before Jin got up, so they hadn't had a chance to talk any more about last night. Even though she hadn't grounded her, it wasn't like Halmoni to just let something serious go. Jin braced herself for whatever scolding her grandmother might be waiting to unleash.

Surprisingly, when Jin reached the counter, Halmoni just nodded at her. "Eat something. You miss dinner yesterday," she said, and stuffed a fried egg sandwich into her granddaughter's hand, as Jin slid into her secret cubby behind the deli counter. It had been less than a week since she'd last visited her special place, but so much had been going on in her life during that time, she'd almost forgotten how good it felt to be here.

Jin took a bite of the sandwich and opened her notebook. Her original plan for this morning was to update and organize her notes, adding the information that she, Alex, and Elvin had learned at Dr. Whitmore's yesterday about Elvin's grandfather and Henriette. But now that she was sitting, cocooned and hidden from the crazy world outside, she didn't feel much like doing that at all. The notes could wait, she decided and opted instead to do a little collecting. Since she started hanging with Alex and Elvin, Jin had seriously been neglecting her "interesting moments" collection. This was a perfect time to record some new moments, ones that were totally unrelated to mysterious attacks and paintings.

After a few minutes of observing a stream of men and women in business suits rushing into the store to grab a newspaper and coffee for the train ride to work, and moms lugging heavy strollers and toddlers stopping to buy snacks for a day at the park, Jin concluded that she hadn't missed much. She started packing up her stuff to get ready for school just as Ameenah Hardwick, who owned the vegetarian restaurant and juice bar a few doors down, sashayed in, wearing a long skirt that swished around her ankles and a gigantic red, green, and yellow head wrap perched on her head like a beacon. In her arms, hugged tightly to her chest, was a stack of orange flyers.

"Good morning, Mrs. Yi," she called to Halmoni. "I'm just making the rounds to remind local business owners about the Harlem World meeting tonight." She peeled a flyer off the top of the stack and placed it on the counter. Halmoni didn't move to pick it up.

Jin's ears perked up as she leaned forward to hear the conversation.

"Councilman Markum is scheduled to lay out his plan for the development. It is of vital importance that we, as entrepreneurs, be there to make our voices heard. We must protect our interests," Ms. Hardwick said, full of passion and indignation.

"What good will it do?" Halmoni exploded. "Markum so sneaky, so full of tricks. Nothing we say will stop him from getting his way."

"I respectfully beg to differ, Mrs. Yi," Ameenah Hardwick argued. "I was just reading in the paper the other day that the mayor's office isn't completely on board with Harlem World. That means that the city council is going to try to delay the vote on this until they get a feel for which way the mayor is leaning on the project. One man should not get to decide what makes Harlem special. I think we still have a shot at convincing them that Harlem World will ruin the fabric of our neighborhood. And besides, we'll never change anything if we don't try."

Halmoni picked up the flyer. "I'll be there," she grumbled, folding and tucking it in her apron pocket.

Great, Jin nearly groaned out loud. Now there was no way she'd get a look at that flyer. Halmoni never took her apron off while she was working, and Jin doubted that she'd voluntarily show it to her, especially since she'd given her a big lecture about avoiding bad guys last night. Jin would have to get her own copy.

She scrambled out from her cubby. "Off to school now. See you later!" she said as she raced past Halmoni.

"Be careful! No stay out late tonight!" Halmoni called after her.

Outside, Jin saw Ameenah Hardwick coming out of a cell phone store across the street. "Miss Hardwick! Miss Hardwick!" She yelled from the curb, pausing to look both ways before darting to the other side. "I was wondering if I could have one of your flyers. I want to take it to school for a project we're doing on our neighborhood," Jin said once she'd caught up with her neighbor.

Ameenah Hardwick beamed. Up close, she smelled of frankincense and oranges, an unexpectedly pleasing combination, Jin noted. She watched Miss Hardwick's head wrap bob and tilt, threatening to topple over as the woman nodded approvingly. "Good for you. I love to meet young people who are involved in making a difference in their community." She handed Jin a flyer.

"Thanks!" Jin said. As she ran off in the opposite direction toward school, she thought about that word: *community*. Harlem was a diverse place full of all sorts of people, but they had one thing in common. They cared about the neighborhood. It really was a special place, and if Miss Hardwick and Halmoni were any indication, Councilman Markum was in for a fight.

"I have something to tell you," Jin and Rose said at the same time. It was later that afternoon and Ms. Weir had given Jin's history class some time to work on their neighborhood projects. Jin, Rose, and Alex had migrated to a table in the back of the classroom so they could work together.

"You go first," Jin said.

"No, you go first." Rose giggled.

"*I'll* go first," Alex huffed. "Yesterday, we went to Elvin's grandfather's apartment and we found something that we'd like you to take a look at." She lowered her voice. "It's a hat," she said, and handed Rose a brown paper shopping bag with the hatbox inside. Rose lifted the lid of the box and peeked at the hat. She let out a loud squeal.

"Girls!" Ms. Weir shot them a sharp glance from the front of the room.

"It's amazing," Rose whispered.

"We need to know everything you can find out about it. But please be careful with it. And you can't tell anyone about this," Alex instructed.

Rose crossed her heart with her index finger. "I promise. It'll be my pleasure to do some research on the hat, but I have one condition. I also get to use my findings for my neighborhood project, which is about Harlem fashion."

"As long as you don't give any details about where it came from, I don't have a problem with that." Alex looked at Jin, who nodded in agreement.

"Yes!" Rose squealed again.

"One more outburst and I'm separating you three," Ms. Weir warned.

"Sorry, Ms. Weir," Rose apologized, and turned back to Jin. "Now what was it that you wanted to tell us?"

Jin reached into her backpack and pulled out the

flyer. "Councilman Markum is holding a community meeting about Harlem World tonight."

Alex grabbed the flyer from Jin. "We are so there!" she said excitedly. "This'll be great for our project. I can't wait to watch Markum squirm."

Jin frowned. "I just have one tiny wrinkle. I think Halmoni is going, and I'm pretty sure she'd be upset if she found out I was there."

"Why? Tell her it's for a school project. She won't mind." Alex shrugged. That was easy for her to say, Jin thought. Alex's parents let her do whatever she wanted.

"It's complicated. I just don't think Halmoni'd be too thrilled to see me at that meeting."

"Well, what if she doesn't *see* you?" Alex proposed. "We'll go after it starts, hang around in the back, and leave right before it's over."

"Maybe," Jin said hesitantly, weighing her options. If Halmoni did see her, she'd probably ground her for the rest of her life. Then again, how could she punish Jin for doing research for school? "I'll think about it."

"I know that I can't go," Rose sighed. "My mom wants me to help her pick out curtains for our new apartment after school today. Which leads me to the thing that I was going to tell you, Jin. I may have found a new owner for Noodles."

"That's awesome, Rose!" Jin grinned.

"Someone at my mom's job mentioned that their sister was interested in getting a dog for her daughter. I emailed her, but she never got back to me. I was wondering if you and Alex could just go by her building to check it out while I'm shopping with my mother. You don't have to talk to anyone or anything, just take a look around to see if it looks like the kind of place where Noodles would be happy. That way I'll know whether or not it's worth reaching out to her again."

"It's a dog. He'll be happy anywhere there's food and a place to poop." Alex rolled her eyes. Jin elbowed her in the side.

"We can do that," she said to Rose.

Rose looked relieved. "Great, I'll text you the address."

If someone had told him a month ago that he would climb up a fire escape, break into an apartment building—while two NYPD cops who were on the lookout *for him* sat outside—and get attacked by two hulking men, Elvin probably would have hid out in his house and refused to leave. But now that he had actually survived a very close encounter with New York City's finest thugs—and sidewalks—Elvin was surprised to find that he didn't feel afraid at all. In fact, he felt brave, and he was itching to do something about it.

Unfortunately, Alex and Jin wouldn't be out of school for another couple of hours, so Elvin had to find something else to do. He'd started by straightening up the apartment. It was way too easy to drop his dishes in the sink and his clothes on the floor when his mother wasn't around to keep him in line. As he picked his coat up off the hallway floor, a piece of paper fluttered out of the pocket. It was the document he'd taken from the printer at the museum the night they'd met Verta Mae Sneed, the one the man he'd seen in the corridor was so eager to get. He'd totally forgotten about it! He sat down where he was to read it, but as soon as he got a good look at it, his hopes for a major clue were dashed. The document turned out to be a list of numbers on a page—nothing about a painting. Maybe the girls could help figure out what they meant.

He went back to cleaning. When he was done, he picked up *The Life of the Invisibles* book and opened it to the first poem.

Invisibility does not equal inanimateness.
That which is invisible lives
In the bricks of buildings warmed by sunlight,
In seedlings sprouting from the earth,
In the breeze that tickles the nose like a feather,
Visible to those who choose to see . . .

Elvin had never been good at poetry. It was his least favorite subject in school. The words in most poems seemed like the writer just randomly picked them and put them next to each other like people squished together on a crowded bus, or worse, was deliberately trying to hide the meaning of the poem, as if it were a secret message or code. *Why couldn't poets just tell you directly what the poems meant?* Elvin thought, his eyes glazing over as he tried to focus.

Frustrated, he tossed the book aside and reached for his phone. Now that he'd finally had the chance to charge it, he turned it on and saw that he'd missed several calls from his mother since the last time they'd spoken a couple days ago. Elvin's entire body tensed, and his hands began to tremble as he pressed the call back button. *"Please be okay, please be okay,"* he whispered. His mother answered after three rings. "Mom!" Elvin cried, relieved.

"Elvin? Where have you been? I've called you at

least ten times. I told you that I worry when I can't reach you," his mom fussed. Her voice sounded a little weak, but Elvin took it as a good sign that she still had enough energy to put him in check.

"Sorry, Mom. I lost my phone. I just found it yesterday."

"Well, you still should've called. How's your grandfather? And why aren't you in school? Your grandfather said he would register you once you settled in. I think it's about time he looked into that."

"We're working on it. But don't worry, I'm definitely learning a lot." Elvin smirked.

"Your grandfather's showing you the city, huh? Sounds like him. He never believed schools were the best place to get an education." His mom's voice trailed off.

"Speaking of education, I found out that he went to medical school," Elvin said. He wondered how much his mother would reveal.

"He told you that?" she asked, surprised.

"Sort of," Elvin hedged. "But what's up with all the secrets, Mom? Why didn't you ever tell me about him? What happened between you two?"

Elvin's mother sighed. "I was hoping to tell you this story in person, but I guess now is as a good a time as any. It might help you to understand your grandfather a little better." She took another deep breath and began. "You know how I've told you that my mother died when I was three years old? She walked in on a guy breaking into an apartment in our building, and in his haste to get away, he pushed her down the stairs and she died from the fall. Your grandfather always blamed himself. He was in medical school at the time, and we lived in a pretty crummy apartment; it was all that he could afford. The landlord never made repairs, and the building was always filthy. The day my mother died, all the hallway lights had blown out. If they had been on, she may have been able to see the burglar and get away. Your grandfather thought he should've fought harder for the landlord to make repairs.

"Shortly afterward, he dropped out of medical school and got involved with some activist artists group. Community service became his life's work. When he wasn't dragging me to meeting after meeting, he was dropping me off with one babysitter or another, most of them his artist friends who also didn't know much about taking care of a kid.

"I became angrier and angrier as I got older. I thought, how could he be so devoted to improving the lives of strangers, and not even care about his own daughter? By the time I turned seventeen, I'd had enough. I had been accepted to Columbia University in New York, but on a whim, I decided to move out to Berkeley with a good friend of mine. I didn't even tell him I was leaving. When I finally got in touch with him to let him know where I was, he just wished me luck and told me that he understood that I had to follow my own path. He wasn't even concerned about what I was doing or how I was surviving. I cut off all communication with him after that. I didn't even tell him when you were born. Maybe I should have . . . though I guess it doesn't matter now. Here you are living with him. Isn't that ironic? Funny how karma can bite you in the butt." His mom chuckled.

"Or maybe I'm a bridge, and I'm supposed to connect the two of you again." Elvin pictured himself stretched from New York to California.

"I like that." Elvin could hear his mom smiling through the phone.

"Mom?"

"Hmm?"

"Thanks for telling me that story."

"You're welcome, honey. I should've told you a long time ago." His mom sounded as if she were drifting off to sleep.

"How are the treatments going?"

"Fine, baby. They just make me a little sleepy."

"Okay, then get some rest. Love you," Elvin whispered as his mom clicked off on the other end. His grandfather and his mom had never been able to understand each other. *Maybe I'm not just a bridge,* he thought. *Maybe I'm the lens that might help them learn to see each other more clearly.* Once his mother was well enough, he'd talk to her about coming to New York for a visit. He'd love to see the city through her eyes, too. For now, all Elvin could do was wait.

And wait Elvin did. When Alex and Jin finally arrived at the apartment after school, they were in a big hurry. Elvin had wanted to discuss the printout he'd taken from the museum, but Alex waved him off. She said she thought she knew what the numbers might mean, and promised to take a closer look later that evening. At the moment, they had more important things to do. They had to check out a prospective new home for Noodles and still make it to the Harlem World community meeting on time. She and Jin had practically dragged Elvin out the door and down the block. And now they seemed lost!

"Are you sure we're in the right place?" Alex stopped in front of a small four-story apartment building on a corner lot.

Jin checked her phone. "This is the address Rose gave me, but it doesn't look like anybody lives here."

The three kids surveyed the building. The front door was boarded up with a flimsy piece of plywood, on which someone had spray painted in red the words *keep out.* None of the windows were covered.

"Look up there." Jin pointed toward the top floor, where one side of the building looked completely normal—there were even curtains and flower boxes in some of the windows. On the other side, however, entire chunks of the upper floors were just gone. Gaping holes and crumbling brick exposed twisted pipes and the wooden frames of missing walls inside.

"It looks like half of the building got hit with a bomb," Elvin observed. "Like when we were studying World War II in school, and our teacher said that sometimes the bombs would hit without warning, and families about to sit down to dinner would have to leave in a hurry, the food and everything still on the table. It's almost like the people who lived here weren't expecting to have to move."

"Those windows, especially the ones with the flowers, are so eerie. It's like seeing a ghost." Jin shuddered. "At least now we know why the woman who was interested in Noodles never emailed Rose again."

Alex shook her head as she paced back and forth in front of the building. "Something's not right here. This is the sloppiest construction site I've ever seen. There aren't any permits, safety signs, or scaffolding. Those loose bricks could fall and hit somebody on the street."

Alex was still pointing out violations when a man approached from behind, startling them.

"You all had people living in this building?" he asked. "Shame what happened to these folks," he continued without waiting for an answer. "A friend of mine who lived here said that one day they had homes, and the next day, literally, the landlord told 'em he'd sold the building and they'd have to move immediately. A lot of those people didn't have nowhere else to go. I heard they started demolition even before the last family was out. Don't seem right, do it?"

"No, sir," Elvin answered for all of them, and the man moved on with a warning to be careful playing around a construction site.

"*Playing?* How old does he think we are? And who would be stupid enough to play at a construction site anyway?" Alex ranted.

Jin ignored her. "What I don't get is how the city of New York could give permission for a building to be demolished if there were still people living there."

"Unless, they didn't," Alex said. "Sometimes people do illegal construction projects without city officials knowing. I heard my dad talking about it. Apparently, it happens all the time."

Just then, they heard a rumbling noise coming from the back of the building, followed by a voice yelling, "Kill the engine! Kill the engine!" Alex, Jin, and Elvin flattened themselves against the side of the building and crept toward the rear. When they reached the end of the wall, they peeked around the corner. The back of the building had been completely knocked out, and they could see now that the entire structure was little more than a hollow shell. A few feet behind the building sat a crane with a large black wrecking ball attached to its long metal arm, its engine idling. The voice sounded again, louder this time. "KILL THE ENGINE!"

The driver turned off the engine and climbed out of the cab, walking toward the building. Alex, Jin, and Elvin ducked out of site. Suddenly, they heard another voice.

"How many times do we have to tell you? We only do demolition after hours and on weekends, when those troublesome building inspectors are off the clock. What part of that don't you get?"

Something about this voice sounded familiar. It was so whiny and wheezy, it grated against Elvin's eardrums. Where had he heard it before?

"These roaches are already upset enough as it is, being forced to move out of here. The last thing we need is one of them calling the city on us," the voice continued.

And then it clicked. *Roaches.* Elvin knew where he'd heard that voice. He turned to Alex and Jin. "I'm going to try to get a closer look. I think I know who that is."

"You can't go by yourself," Jin whispered.

"Yeah, we're going with you," Alex insisted.

Elvin rolled his eyes and started inching forward. "It sounds like they're inside the building," he said. They tiptoed to the back of the building and darted into the first opening they found. Jin took a quick look around. They were in what used to be an apartment. She guessed that they were standing in the kitchen because there was a large white sink with a countertop and cabinet underneath near the wall in one corner.

"Go on, get outta here. We'll call you if we need you," they heard the whiny voice snap.

"The voices are coming from the next apartment," Elvin whispered. They waited until they heard the heavy footsteps of the crane operator exit the building, before creeping closer to the wall separating the two apartments, which was still intact except for a fist-sized hole near the middle. A pile of lumber was stacked at the base of the wall beneath the opening.

"I think if I stand on the wood, I can see through the opening to the other side," Elvin estimated.

Alex eyed the wood suspiciously. "I don't know, it doesn't look that sturdy," she said, but Elvin was already scaling the pile. When he got to the top, he found that his head didn't quite reach the opening. *Why do I have to be so short?* he sighed to himself.

Alex scanned the room for something to add to the pile that would lift Elvin up a few more inches. "There's more lumber over there." She pointed across the room.

As Jin and Alex went to get the wood, Elvin pressed his ear to the wall. He could hear two men talking.

"How could you have made so many mistakes?" a new voice boomed, deep and stern. "How could you have let that kid discover the painting? The garden was on the list. That should have been us. And then the old man gave you nothing."

"I didn't let anyone do anything," the whiny voice complained. "And besides, if it wasn't for that kid, we wouldn't have even known about the painting."

The other man ignored him. "And don't get me started on the apartment . . ."

At that moment, Jin and Alex were sizing up a pile of damp lumber. Jin touched the two boards

closest to them with the tip of her sneaker. Alex nodded. Jin tucked the notebook she'd been carrying
beneath her armpit, and the two of them bent to pick
up the wood. Once they lifted it, Jin saw hundreds of
black spots, one on top the other, covering the space
where they'd just removed the wood, and on the
pieces of wood that they were carrying. When one of
those spots started to crawl, just inches from her fingers, she let go of her end of the wood, sending it
clattering to the floor.

"What the . . . why'd you drop it?" Alex shot her
a look. Jin pointed frantically.

"Ants!" she panted, trying her best to swallow the
scream that was mounting in her throat. "Ants!"
When Alex saw the squirming black spots, she threw
the wood down with a loud *thunk!* and started hop-
ping around wildly, shaking out her long black jacket.

Next door, the men stopped talking. "What was
that?" one of them asked.

Elvin scrambled down the pile of lumber. "They're
coming! We have to hide," he said, and ran toward
the kitchen sink and pantry in the corner with Jin
and Alex right behind him.

Once they were safely hidden, Jin realized that in
her haste, she'd made a terrible mistake. "My notebook, it's out there," she whispered hoarsely as blood

rushed to her ears and her neck got hot with panic. She peered around the edge of the sink. Her pale pink notebook lay, exposed and vulnerable, on the floor in the middle of the room. And now, as the two men from next door came charging into the room, it was too late to rescue it.

From his hiding spot in the cabinet underneath the sink, Elvin nudged open one of the cabinet doors so he could peek at the men. The one he could see was shaped like a pumpkin, squat and round, with a bald head, thick glasses, and freckles dotting his yellow-tinted skin. Elvin felt a jolt of recognition. He had seen the same round shape and heard the same whiny voice at the Studio Museum. And now he'd heard the guy mention an old man—that had to be Elvin's grandfather!

"It was probably just a rat," the whiny voiced man said, swiveling his head to inspect the room. Elvin tried to get a look at the other man, but he could only see small pieces of him—a hand here, a pant leg there. One thing did stick out, though: a pair of pointy-toed olive-colored animal-skin boots. Maybe alligator or snake, Elvin guessed.

"Well, you and your flunky better get it together," the man said as he paced. "We can't afford any more mistakes." The man tripped over something, then stopped suddenly, and a momentary hush fell over the room. After a long moment, he turned to his partner and said, "Let's get out of here."

Elvin, Jin, and Alex all held their breath as the sound of the men's footsteps got farther and farther away. When they were sure the men were gone, they climbed out from their hiding places. Jin ran to retrieve her notebook. It was nowhere to be found.

"They took it!" she cried. "It had all our notes. This is terrible." Fat tears rolled down her cheeks.

"It'll be okay," Alex said, patting her arm awkwardly. "They probably won't understand what it all means, and besides, we already know everything in that notebook. And they'll never be able to connect us to it." Jin nodded, but she still felt pretty awful. Losing her notebook was like losing a limb.

"This might not be the right time to say this, but don't we have a Harlem World meeting to get to?" Elvin asked shyly.

"The meeting!" Alex said, turning to Jin. "Are you feeling up to going?"

Jin nodded firmly. She wasn't going to let losing a notebook stop her from helping Elvin and possibly saving her neighborhood.

As they crept toward the hole in the brick where

they'd entered the building, Elvin heard the motor of the crane starting up. "I thought they said they weren't doing any demolition now?" As they slipped through the exit, a sharp whistle pierced the air. Elvin looked up just in time to see the wrecking ball swinging in their direction. "Run!" he shouted.

They didn't stop until they were several blocks away.

"They must've seen us," Elvin gasped, doubled over, struggling to catch his breath.

"And they have my notebook," Jin groaned. "This is not good."

"Let's keep it together, people!" Alex snapped. "We just need to find Henriette's missing paintings before those guys do."

"I did find out one thing," Elvin offered as they began to walk. "Both of those men knew about the paintings—they mentioned them when they were talking. And I recognized one of them. He was at the museum, and I think he was also in my grandfather's apartment that night. What if he had a hand in the attack?"

"This is major!" Jin said, reaching for her notebook, which, of course, wasn't there.

"Now all we have to do is figure out his angle. What's the motive? How do all these pieces fit together?

Easy peasy, right?" Alex said, so charged-up that she practically started skipping down the street.

"Yeah, right," Jin and Elvin grumbled, trailing behind her. They'd just had their second near-death experience in a week, and, unlike Alex, neither of them was looking forward to the prospect of more.

The Abyssinian Baptist Church rose like a sentinel from its prominent perch on 138th Street, looking every bit the majestic Harlem monument that it was. As the first African American Baptist church in New York, Abyssinian had weathered its share of neighborhood changes: battles for territory and civil rights, conflicts among community members, and also, on occasion, reconciliations. It was only fitting that a meeting about Harlem World, a development that could have a significant impact on the neighborhood, be held here, in this historic place.

By the time Alex, Elvin, and Jin arrived, the church was packed, wall to wall, with people coming to state their case and voice their grievances. The air in the church was thick with heat and humidity generated by so many bodies crowded together. The three kids pushed their way through the doors and slid into the last available space along the back wall. Jin scanned the crowd for Halmoni. She caught sight of her grandmother's frizzy, curly hair in a pew near the front of the church. Then she noticed her grandfather, standing close to where Halmoni was sitting, shaking hands and chatting with their neighbors.

"Uh-oh, double trouble. Both of my grandparents are here," Jin whispered to Alex, jutting her chin in her grandparents' direction. "Keep your eye on Halmoni's hair. If that hair moves, we're out of here."

Alex nodded and turned her attention to the front of the room, where Ameenah Hardwick was stepping onto the pulpit. She wore a long black skirt and another gigantic head wrap, this one made of a gauzy white material. She cleared her throat and began to speak, projecting her voice to the back of the room.

"Good evening, brothers and sisters, fellow business owners, and neighbors. My name is Ameenah Hardwick, and I am president of the Alliance of Harlem Business Owners. We are gathered here this evening to discuss a matter of great importance to our community. Councilman Geld Markum has asked for an opportunity to present his ideas for a new development in our neighborhood. Let us be respectful and hear him out. There will be time for questions following his presentation."

Ameenah Hardwick stepped off the pulpit, and as she passed Markum, she pretended not to see his outstretched hand. People began to shift in their seats and whisper loudly. One couple even booed while Markum and his assistant set up for his presentation.

"Good evening, Harlem!" Markum's voice boomed through the microphone. "I'm here to talk to you about what I believe is an amazing opportunity for Harlem. I was born and raised in this neighborhood, and I still live here, so I know what we need to make this an even better place than it already is. Imagine all of Harlem's historic riches on display for the world to see. Places like Colonial Williamsburg and Greenfield Village may showcase important aspects of American history, but they don't have anything on us! We have Langston Hughes and the Harlem Renaissance, the Apollo Theater, and the Cotton Club. And I've designed the Harlem World development to be a win-win situation for all of us." A slide with a series of graphs and pie charts popped up on the screen behind him. "As you can see, we anticipate that Harlem World will significantly increase tourism to our area, which will lead to more jobs for Harlem residents, and a spike in revenue for local business owners."

"That's only if we get to stay open!" Jin watched Mr. Adibisi, who owned the dry cleaner's a few storefronts down from the bodega, stand so he could be heard. "I hear you're planning on shutting down a lot of businesses."

Markum plastered a fake smile on his face, which barely hid his sneer. "The goal, my friend, is to increase opportunities for all. Will there be some changes? Of course. But these changes will lead to more jobs and more money for more members of our community. Now, if you'll turn your attention to this next slide, I'd like to share with you some details about the development." A slide with an illustration of a multi-colored blob, shaped like a peanut, appeared on the screen.

"I've designed Harlem World to be a series of theme parks within a theme park, each location honoring a different facet of Harlem's rich culture and history." Markum grabbed a small pointer and shined a red laser dot on the illustration. "This, as you can probably guess by its indigo color, is Ellingtonia, named for the great Duke Ellington and his famous song, 'Mood Indigo.' This is where we'll have our jazz-themed rides, including the high-speed 'Bird' roller coaster, named in honor of Charlie Parker, as well as three world-class jazz performance venues. Over here, in orange, is the Harlem Renaissance Faire—"

"What about the little guy?" Mr. Adibisi interrupted. "I don't hear anything about us."

Markum kept his cool. "Sir, there will be plenty of opportunities for small business owners. If you would just wait until the Q and A portion of this presentation, I will do my best to address your concerns."

Mr. Adibisi ignored him and rose to his feet again. He was dressed in traditional African attire, with a long flowing shirt and pants, and had a thick gray beard and dreadlocks that went down to his knees. "I don't believe you. You people come in here with all your fancy talk and promises, and who gets obliterated? The little guy, the small business owners who are the backbone of this community."

"Yeah!" shouted Mr. Morales, a teacher at Jin and Alex's school. "Look at what happened with the Magic Skillet!" For once, Markum appeared flustered, his cool demeanor coming apart at the seams. He glanced over at Ameenah Hardwick for help, but she just looked away. Suddenly, a hush fell over the audience as Miss Norma—a longtime Harlem resident and local legend—made her way to the front of the room, her cane clicking against the floor.

"How dare you insult us with such a preposterous plan. An amusement park?" she spat. "The people of

Harlem are not pawns to be used for your amuse-ment. And besides, who says new is better? Who says shiny and fast and big make a community viable? *We* do that. The people who live and work here. We can't let some politician come in here and paint us out of the picture, or keep building on top of us, around us, or over us until we completely disappear. This community is our home. We will not allow you to come into our neighborhood and render us invisible!" The room erupted in applause as Ameenah Hardwick led Miss Norma back to her seat.

Alex hooted and applauded with the rest of the crowd. Out of the corner of her eye, she saw Halmoni and Harabeoji getting up and nudged Jin with her elbow. "Your grandparents are leaving," she shouted above the noise. The three kids quickly shoved their way through the crowd toward the exit. At the door, Alex grabbed an information packet from a Harlem World representative.

Jin rushed ahead. "I know we have a lot to talk about, but I can't let Halmoni see me here. I'll talk to you guys tomorrow!" she called over her shoulder. As she raced home, Jin thought about Miss Norma's words. And she remembered what Verta Mae had told them about how the Invisible 7 had worked to help people better their community. It occurred to her that their work wasn't just about getting people involved and painting cool pictures. It was about *refusing* to be invisible. It was about being seen. It was high time someone took up that cause, and in Jin's mind, tonight had been a very good start.

Alex stormed into Elvin's apartment the next day and threw two pieces of paper down on the coffee table, before dunking an apple slice into the jar of peanut butter and stuffing it into her mouth. "The news isn't good," she said solemnly once she'd finished chewing.

"What news?" Elvin asked.

Alex pointed to the papers on the coffee table. "I looked through some of my dad's real estate stuff and figured out what the numbers on the list from the museum mean. They're borough, block, and lot, also known as BBL numbers. Every property in New York has one. The city uses BBL numbers to identify the location of buildings, and also for property taxes and stuff like that."

"So by looking at the BBL number, can you figure out the address of a particular piece of property?" Jin asked, opening to the first page of a new notebook. Alex nodded. "Which means that all the numbers on our list correspond to specific addresses?" Alex nodded again.

"I don't see how that helps us," Elvin said. "Even if we know the addresses, that still doesn't tell us why they're on that museum guy's list in the first place."

"I thought so, too. But then I started noticing that all the addresses were in Harlem, and all of them were located in a pretty defined area of the neighborhood," Alex explained. "All of them also happen to be located in the Harlem World development zone. Which means that Museum Guy might be working with Markum. And Markum could be planning to bulldoze the properties on the list to make way for his stupid theme park."

Jin sighed heavily. "This is awful," she said.

"It gets worse." Alex shook her head. "The partially demolished building we checked out yesterday, the community garden, the Magic Skillet, they were all on the list."

"So that's what he meant." Elvin's brain clicked. "Yesterday at the building, those guys were arguing about Jarvis finding the painting in the garden, and one of them mentioned that the garden was on the list. Now I get it." He sat down on the couch, holding his head in his hands as the reality of what he'd just said sank in. "These awful things, my grandfather's attack, the Magic Skillet closing, the building being demolished were all planned. Whoever did it meant to destroy those places. They meant to hurt people."

Alex sat down beside him. "Don't be sad, Elvin. We're gonna stop them. I promise."

"But—but I thought that Markum had to wait to get approval for the project before starting any demolition," Jin sputtered.

Alex shrugged. "Either he's really confident that he's going to get approval and giving himself a major head start on the building process, or else he just doesn't care."

"We need to go to the police! This has gone too far. We can't let Markum get away with this," Jin said, outraged.

Elvin's head jerked up. "He *is* getting away with it! Markum has that museum guy working for him, and they tried to kill us yesterday," he said, his voice rising in pitch. "And I don't mean to sound paranoid here, but who's to say that the police aren't also working for the councilman? They're already looking for me. Could this whole mess get any worse?"

"Well, yes, actually," Alex piped up, on cue. "Harlem Hospital is also on Markum's list. Sorry."

"What?" Elvin whirled around to face her. "When are they planning to tear it down?" he demanded.

"That's the thing, we don't know. The list only has the addresses, not the construction schedule."

Elvin stood up abruptly and hurriedly put on his grandfather's bulky trench coat and baseball hat.

"Where are you going?" Alex asked.

"I'm going to the hospital to check on my grandfather. You're welcome to come if you'd like," he said as he flew out the door.

* • *

The main lobby of Harlem Hospital was bustling. Patients and doctors rushed to get to appointments. Orderlies swerved wheelchairs among the crowd, threatening knees and toes. Families huddled around sick loved ones, and elderly couples leaned on one another as they slowly tottered through the throng.

"Hey, there's Henriette's mural! The one Dr. Whitmore told us about." Jin pointed excitedly to a large mural that nearly took up an entire wall on the other side of the lobby. "Let's go check it out."

"Wait! We have to find out about my grandfather first," Elvin said.

"Okay, but how do we do that? I don't think it's safe for you to ask anyone about him," Jin said.

"There's an information desk over there. I'll go

and see if they'll tell me anything about his condition," Alex volunteered.

Jin and Elvin watched as Alex casually walked toward the desk. "She's not afraid of anything," Jin said softly. Even though Alex could be reckless, Jin admired her courage, which definitely came in handy in times like these.

Elvin did not agree. "A little fear never hurt anyone," he said, pulling his baseball hat further down on his head. "I hope she doesn't blow our cover and have the entire hospital staff after us."

Alex had no idea what she was going to say as she approached the information desk, which was staffed by a woman sporting platinum-blond hair with bright pink streaks. It was a terrible dye job, Alex noted. She could clearly see the woman's dark roots, like a bed of soil beneath the brassy blond strands. "Excuse me," Alex said politely.

"Can I help you?" The woman asked without looking up from the magazine she was hunched over.

"I was wondering if you could give me some information about a patient."

The woman sighed and reluctantly tore her eyes away from the magazine. "Name?"

"Jacob Morrow."

Turning to her keyboard, the woman typed in the

name with three-inch nails, painted the exact same shade of pink as the color in her hair. "You family?"

"I'm his niece."

The woman glanced up at her suspiciously. "Says here his only family is the grandson who brought him in. I can only give patient information to the family members we have in our system," she said. Then she quickly peeked over her shoulder and leaned toward Alex. "Normally, I'd give you the information, but my supervisor's right over there and she's been breathing down my neck today," the woman whispered.

So your supervisor is cool with you reading a magazine on duty? Alex wanted to say, but she just thanked the woman and headed back over to Jin and Elvin. Instead of stopping where they were, she kept walking past them, beckoning them to follow her into a crowded elevator bank. She didn't want to risk anyone spotting Elvin.

"What did she say?" Elvin asked.

"She wouldn't tell me anything. You're the only family member listed," Alex said.

"Now what?" Jin asked.

Alex watched a crowd of people pushing onto an elevator. "Hey, do you remember your grandfather's room number?" she asked Elvin. Elvin gave her the number, and before they could stop her, Alex jumped onto the elevator. "Meet you at the mural in a few minutes!" she called as the doors snapped shut.

Jin and Elvin quickly made their way over to Henriette's mural. The large painting depicted a vibrant, colorful scene of a block in Harlem. Through the windows of brownstones, the viewer could see scenes of the lives of residents inside. There was a family eating a meal together, a jazz musician practicing his horn, a little girl doing her schoolwork. In one window, a woman sat crying in a chair, while others hovered around to comfort her. In the next apartment, a child slept, cradling a stuffed animal beneath its chin. In another scene, a burglar snuck out of an apartment, carrying a sack of stolen goods on his back. Outside of the buildings, a little boy tottered on a rocking horse, surrounded by bigger boys riding bikes and playing ball. At the other end of the block, a group of girls clustered around a game of jacks on the sidewalk, while another younger girl skipped rope off by herself. In between, neighbors gathered, talking and laughing on front stoops.

Making the invisible visible, Jin thought, remembering Miss Norma's speech. "This piece is amazing, isn't it?" she said to Elvin as she took a step toward the painting to get a closer look. She saw an elaborate black feather in the lower right corner of the mural that she hadn't noticed before. It made the piece feel darker, sadder, somehow. "That's odd. Why would someone put a feather there?" she muttered. "Doesn't it look out of place?" she asked Elvin.

"Yeah," Elvin answered absently, his eyes drawn to a sudden rush of activity near the elevator banks. "Speaking of things being out of place, what are they doing here?" he asked nervously.

Jin followed his gaze. Councilman Markum strode confidently down the hall, surrounded by a tight cluster of associates and reporters, Verta Mae Sneed among them. "So she is working with Markum," she said, pointing her out to Elvin.

"And look, there's Museum Guy." Elvin shuddered as he nodded toward a rotund man whose pudgy legs struggled to keep up with Markum.

Jin and Elvin flattened themselves against the wall. As they waited for the group to pass, Jin overheard two nearby janitors commenting on the entourage.

"They brought out the bigwigs today. All for a *painting*, can you believe it?" said one of the men, who was pushing a cart loaded with cleaning supplies. Jin nudged Elvin, who nodded to let her know that he was listening.

"That *painting*, my friend, could save us our jobs," the other man retorted, swishing around his mop to emphasize the point. "I, for one, thank the man upstairs that that kid found it. I heard the hospital is claiming that they own it, and it's worth a lot of money. Might just save this place."

How would Harlem Hospital own a painting by Henriette that was buried in a garden? Jin wondered.

"I don't think they're really going to close this place," the first janitor argued. "This is a Harlem institution. Where else are the people gonna go when they get sick?"

"What planet are you living on? With the way things are going, this place could be gone tomorrow. That Markum guy has got the higher-ups salivating over his Harlem World project, saying that he's gonna fund a state-of-the art medical facility that would make this place look like a dinosaur."

"Don't they know that the past doesn't die? It lives beneath and just blossoms into new forms again and again. I read that somewhere," the janitor with the cart said.

"Maybe you oughta give Markum a copy of that book," the man with the mop joked. The two men chuckled as they moved down the hallway.

A few minutes later, Alex appeared. "And the Academy Award for Best Performance, goes to . . .

moi!" she exploded. "You should've seen it. I did my best pathetic kid routine."

"Alex," Jin tried to interrupt her.

Alex ignored her. "I was peeking into your grandfather's room when one of the nurses saw me. Immediately, I pretended like I was about to start crying. *He's my favorite uncle! I don't know what I'll do if he dies!* I really laid it on. I think the nurse just gave me the info to shut me up." She turned to Elvin. "Your grandfather's still in a coma, but he's stable."

"Thanks, I appreciate it," Elvin mumbled, his eyes darting to look at Jin.

"What's going on?" Alex asked.

"The painting is here. Markum and his entourage just left. Verta Mae Sneed was with them," Jin filled her in, and also told her about the janitors' conversation that they'd overheard.

Alex's mouth dropped open. "We've got to get a look at that painting."

"Exactly," Jin said. "Markum and his crew came from over here." She pointed and led the way.

The painting was in a small rotunda in a newer section of the hospital. The area was roped off with a sign posted at the entrance that said PRIVATE. There was a glass case in the center of the enclosed area. A beefy security guard stood watch. Elvin, Alex, and Jin ducked back around the corner before he could see them.

"The painting must be in that case," Alex said.

"But how do we get past the guard? That guy looks like he could squish us with one hand," Elvin whispered.

"I have an idea," Jin said. "You two go up to the guard and ask him a question, something like how to get to the nearest vending machine. If he steps away from his post to show you, I'll sneak in and take some shots of the painting."

Alex and Elvin agreed and approached the guard. Just as Jin suspected, the guard stepped away to point them down a nearby corridor. She quickly ducked under the rope barricade and ran over to the glass case. There was a canvas stretched out inside, but Jin didn't stop to look at it, she just started snapping pictures with her phone.

"Hey!" She heard a booming voice behind her. "You can't be in this area." The security guard marched toward her.

Jin took a step back. "Uh, no speak English," she said in a thick, generic Asian accent, and bowed her head slightly for full effect. People saw what they wanted to see, and for once, Jin was happy to use a ridiculous stereotype to her advantage.

"YOU CANNOT BE IN THIS AREA!" he shouted, and waved his arms in wild circular motions, shaking his head violently at the same time.

She nearly laughed out loud. If she really didn't speak his language, did he think talking louder would make her suddenly understand him?

"So. No photo?" Jin said.

"YOU HAVE TO LEAVE!" He ushered her down the corridor where Elvin and Alex had disappeared. Jin found them munching on a bag of chips from the vending machine. Jin's legs wobbled. Her nerves were only now catching up with her.

"Did it work?" Alex asked. Jin nodded and handed over her phone.

Alex flipped through the pictures, frowning. "We still don't know the significance of this piece, or even if it's really Henriette's. I think we need Rad to weigh in on this one."

Jin rolled her eyes, annoyed. *I did all that, and she just brushes it off like it doesn't matter?*

Elvin fell into step beside her. "Nice work back there. Celebratory chip?" he offered.

"Fine," Jin snapped as she grabbed the package and downed the entire bag.

CHAPTER 16

Jin still felt irritated ten minutes later as they waited for Rad in the cereal aisle of a grocery store, a block away from the hospital. "Do we really have to meet him here?"

"I just wanted to be safe. Hospital security might still be on the lookout for Elvin," Alex answered.

"So now you want to be safe?" Jin muttered under her breath. *I pretty much just risked my life, not to mention what would happen to me if Halmoni found out, just to take a picture of a stupid painting—and Alex hasn't said a word about it. It must only matter when she and Rad do cool, dangerous stuff,* Jin thought, contorting her face into a frown.

"What did you say?" Alex glanced at her. "Are you okay?"

"I'm fine," Jin huffed, and picked up a box of Cap'n Crunch.

"No, seriously. You seem upset," Alex pressed.

"I said I'm fine." Jin pretended to be totally engrossed in the list of ingredients on the side of the box.

"Suit yourself," Alex said, and wandered to the other end of the aisle, where she plopped down onto the floor and started swiping away at her phone. A few seconds later, Rad rolled into the aisle on his skateboard.

"I prefer Frosted Flakes, but Cap'n Crunch will do in a pinch," he joked, tapping the box Jin was holding as he hopped off his board. "What up, dudes?"

Alex mumbled a weak "hey," and Jin just nodded slightly in response.

"Whoa, I'm getting some serious negative vibes here. What's going on?" Rad glanced at Elvin, who gave him a bewildered shrug.

"Ask Jin," Alex muttered.

"I said I was fine," Jin snapped.

"Hold up, dudes! Look around you. Do you see where you are?" Rad gestured toward the colorful boxes lining the shelves. "This is the cereal aisle. This is a happy place. Whatever is going on here, you need to squash it."

"Jin is the one who's upset." Alex stood up and walked back to the group.

"Well, I wouldn't be upset if *someone* didn't think that she deserved all the credit for everything."

"Are you talking about me? How could you even say that?" Alex looked genuinely hurt.

"For one, you always want us to say how great the stuff you do is, but you never say the same for other people. Like just now, you bragged about sneaking up to Elvin's grandfather's hospital room, but when I snuck past that guard to take the picture of the painting, you didn't say anything." Jin folded her arms across her chest.

"Maybe because I thought it went without saying how brilliant an idea that was."

"Well, it doesn't. Go without saying, that is."

Alex raised both arms above her head. "Hear ye! Hear ye! Let the record show that I think Jin Yi is a brilliant mastermind, a sleuth of the highest order. This I proclaim to all those far and wide, now and forevermore!" Alex grinned and turned to Jin. "Seriously, I do think you're brilliant. Happy now?"

A smile crept across Jin's face. "It's a start," she said.

"As the great Chinese philosopher Lao Tzu said, 'The journey of a thousand miles begins with one step.' Awesome work here, dudes." Rad held out both hands and Jin and Alex gave him a fist bump. "Now, let's move on to the painting. Lay it on me."

Jin handed him her phone. Rad squinted at the screen for several long minutes.

"Since you guys asked me about Henriette

Drummond, I've been doing some research on her and the work of the Invisible 7. They were a pretty amazing group of artists. This piece definitely looks like it could be one of Henriette's, but it doesn't seem finished to me. It looks almost like a study for a larger work," Rad said.

"Maybe another mural?" Jin wondered, reaching for the phone. She studied the image of the painting. Rad was right, the piece did look more like a sketch. Comprised of a series of miniature black-and-white portraits, it didn't have the colorful and expressive figures and backgrounds the hospital mural had. Most of the people in the painting were doctors and nurses dressed in white coats and uniforms, others were dressed in more traditional attire from Africa, Asia, and India. She remembered what Dr. Whitmore had told them about how Henriette had destroyed the sketches after she finished the Harlem Hospital mural. *Maybe this sketch was for a mural she never got to paint,* Jin thought.

"'The Healers,'" Elvin read the title of the piece over Jin's shoulder. "Wait, why is that person holding a human heart?" He pointed to one of the figures. Jin looked closely and saw that the person was indeed cradling a heart, small as a bird in his hands. Another person held a brain, and yet another, a pair of eyes.

Most of the people in the portraits held less unusual items, like stethoscopes, plants, or a mortar and pestle.

"The Invisible 7 painted a lot of murals that celebrated regular people from the neighborhood, and also those who they felt had made a contribution to the community," Rad explained. "Usually, they included some symbol of that person's field or specialty in the painting," Rad explained. "So that dude with the heart was maybe an awesome heart surgeon."

"Hey, there's Dr. Whitmore, without his beard." Elvin pointed and read the name below one of the figures. "He's holding a baby."

"Yeah, he was an obstetrician before he retired," Alex chimed. "I'll have to tell him we saw this. The Invisible 7 seem like they were pretty cool."

"I thought you guys might be into them. I also found several other Invisible 7 murals around the neighborhood. Those dudes really were about something, you know?" Rad said.

"Will you show us the other murals?" Alex asked.

Rad broke into a wide grin. "I was hoping you'd ask. Lately, I've been kind of obsessed with the 'Sevens'—that's what I started calling them. I even came up with my own little Invisible 7 mural walking tour. You dudes can be my first customers." Jin looked over at him, surprised. Even she had to give Rad credit. Skater Dude had designed *a walking tour.*

After buying a box of Frosted Flakes for the road, they headed for the first stop on the tour. Rad rolled ahead on his board, while Alex, Elvin, and Jin trailed behind on foot.

"I might have to make this a skateboard tour in the future. That way everyone can stay together," Rad said when the three of them had finally caught up with him in front of the former Magic Skillet restaurant.

Alex peered through the large front window into the now empty diner. "We've got to stop Markum," she whispered to Jin, who nodded in agreement.

"It is a real bummer that this fine establishment is closed," Rad said. "But at least there's a really cool mural that will allow its legacy to live on. Follow me." He led them across the street to a large mural painted on the side of another building, and pulled a crumpled piece of paper out of his pocket. "This mural actually pays homage to both the Magic Skillet and the Harlem YMCA. You can see the images of people eating at the Skillet and then doing stuff at the Y, which not only gave people a place to live but also hosted a lot of cultural activities. There was even a theater company here at one point," Rad read from his notes on the paper. "The Skillet and the Y were both really important institutions that nourished the people of Harlem," he said, sounding like a real tour guide.

Jin noticed a feather painted in the lower right-hand corner of the mural. It was just like the black one she'd seen on the mural at the hospital, except this one was bright green. "What's with the feather?" she asked.

"Oh, that's the logo of the Invisible 7. It's on all their work, so that's how you know the piece is one of theirs. Sometimes, instead of an entire mural, they'd just paint the feather on a particular building, to honor a person or organization." Rad consulted his notes again. "They believed art had the power to speak to people directly. The feather is supposed to symbolize hope and freedom," he read.

"Didn't we see that feather in Verta Mae Sneed's office?" Elvin asked.

That's right! Jin suddenly remembered the red banner with the green feather hanging behind Verta Mae Sneed's desk. She'd even made a sketch of it in her notebook—the notebook the developers from the building now had in their possession. She felt a wave of nausea churn in her stomach and inch up her esophagus at the thought. *Focus on the future, focus on the future,* she repeated to herself until the queasiness went away, then opened the new notebook she'd brought and quickly jotted down a question:

If the invisible 7 feather is green, why is the one on the hospital mural black?

"All right, dudes, let's roll!" Rad hopped on his board, ready to move on. They traveled uptown to an elegant townhome on Hamilton Terrace, where there was a single feather painted above the door. "This used to be the home of jazz singer Mary Lou Williams, who you probably never heard of—but check her out. She turned this house into a twenty-four-hour jazz academy. Lots of famous jazz musicians came here to study," Rad said.

Next, they visited a mural that celebrated the Last Poets, a group of spoken-word artists from the 1960s who used poetry as a means to speak out against injustice, Rad told them. "These dudes were like rappers before there were rappers. They inspired hip-hop. Pretty awesome," he gushed.

They visited several more murals, depicting a wide range of scenes, from parent protests for better schools for their kids to neighbors cleaning up their blocks, before coming to their last stop, a small brick building on 122nd Street and 7th Avenue. "It's an abandoned church now, and way back in the day, it used to be a carriage house and stable for the owners of the brownstones in the area. But most important, this building was the original meeting place of the Invisible 7. This is where it all began, where the magic happened." Rad stared reverently at the crumbling building, while Elvin, Jin, and Alex moved in closer.

"It's not exactly welcoming," Alex said, taking a look around.

"Hey, look at this!" Elvin pointed at a carved stone head of a goat, posted like a sentry above the building's entrance. "This is some kind of crazy coincidence." He pulled the goat Pez dispenser his grandfather had given him out of his pocket. Ever since the attack, he'd taken to carrying it around with him.

"Something tells me it's not a coincidence," Jin remarked, making a few notes. "Maybe it's some kind of message."

Elvin frowned. "If the message is that my grand-father is stubborn, I've already gotten it loud and clear."

"Cheer up, dude!" Rad clapped Elvin on the shoulder. "I have one more thing to show you guys," he said.

They hopped on the subway back uptown to 135th Street, where Rad led them into the Schomburg

Center for Research in Black Culture. "This is one of best research libraries in the city. Oh, and the ashes of the poet Langston Hughes are also buried here, literally right here," he said, pointing to the floor as they walked through a small atrium. Jin sped up. As much as she enjoyed reading Langston Hughes's poetry, she wasn't crazy about the idea of walking on his ashes.

Rad led them down a stairwell to one of the research rooms.

"Hello, Radley," said a man sitting at a desk at the entrance of the room. Rad blushed and immediately spun around to give his three companions a stony glare. "Not a word about the name," he hissed, then turned back to the librarian. "Hey, Mr. Bell. I was wondering if you could pull the file that I was working on the last time I was here, the one about the Invisible 7."

Mr. Bell handed Rad a materials request slip, which he quickly filled out. Then Mr. Bell disappeared into a room behind the desk. He reappeared shortly and handed Rad a slim file folder. Rad found a table for the four of them.

"From what I can tell, the Invisible 7 broke up in the late 1960s, and it seemed to have something to do with this exhibit at the Metropolitan Museum of Art in 1969 called *Harlem on My Mind*," Rad said once they were all seated. "This was supposed to be an exhibit that celebrated the culture and history of Harlem, which, on the surface, seemed like a really good idea, totally in line with the work that the Invisible 7 was doing around the neighborhood, right? But somehow, this thing went south really fast and exploded into a major controversy," he explained. "Henriette and the Invisible 7 were among the most visible protestors of the exhibit." Rad took a piece of paper out of the folder and slid it onto the table.

Jin reached for it. "'An Open Letter to the Metropolitan Museum of Art and the Curators of the *Harlem on My Mind* Exhibition,'" she read aloud. "'We, the artists and members of the Invisible 7, respectfully protest the aforementioned exhibition on the following grounds:

1. The Museum has refused to allow residents of Harlem to have any meaningful input or participation in the planning of the *Harlem on My Mind* exhibition.

2. The *Harlem on My Mind* exhibition does not accurately, or adequately, represent the work of Harlem artists. Furthermore, the exhibit includes only photographs.

Painters and artists of other visual media are completely overlooked and excluded.

" 'We demand that the museum take immediate steps to incorporate the voices of the Harlem community, or halt all planning and production of this exhibit. Signed, the Invisible 7,' " Jin finished reading.

"So what happened next?" Alex asked.

"Not too much." Rad shook his head. "The museum went ahead with the exhibit as planned. But here's where it gets interesting. The night before the exhibit opened, there was some kind of fancy party at the Met. At some point during the event, somebody vandalized some of the other paintings in the museum's collection by scratching the letter *H* into the canvases. They even got one by that famous painter dude, Rembrandt. Talk about tagging." Rad winked at Elvin before continuing.

"The paintings weren't seriously damaged, but, still, it was a pretty major deal. There were loads of protestors outside the museum during the event, but folks suspected someone on the inside," he explained.

Alex flipped through the papers in Rad's file, pausing to read one of them. "It says here that Henriette was one of a select group of painters who'd been invited to participate in some kind of fellowship program that the Met was sponsoring for promising young artists," she reported.

"Exactly!" Rad clapped his hands. "Most of the people in the Harlem arts community, including the Invisible 7, thought that Henriette vandalized those paintings. She had the motive and the opportunity. And get this, she never denied doing it."

"But why? Why would she throw away such a prestigious opportunity? I bet most artists would kill to have a fellowship at the Metropolitan Museum." Jin raised her voice. She couldn't help but feel outraged by what she saw as a frivolous act on Henriette's part.

"Prestige isn't everything," Alex argued.

"That's kinda what Henriette said. Read this," Rad held out another article.

"Though not formally charged, artist Henriette Drummond is a person of interest in the egregious act of vandalism that damaged ten paintings from the Metropolitan Museum's collection," Alex read aloud. "The crime is believed to have occurred during a gala at the Met, celebrating the opening of the controversial *Harlem on My Mind* exhibition.

"When asked for comment, museum staff member, Verta Mae Sneed, a key researcher and advisor for the exhibition, had this to say: 'This horrendous event has damaged not only great works of art, but also the relationship between some members of the Harlem art community and the Metropolitan Museum. The museum has asked Miss Drummond to leave our fellowship program and declines to pursue further action at this time. We want to move forward and heal from this tragedy.'"

"Speaking on her own behalf, Miss Drummond said simply, 'When you take art away from the people, you also take away their ability to tell their own stories, to shape their own destinies.'"

Rad closed his folder. "And that's it. There weren't any new murals after that. I think the Invisible 7 just kind of broke up. Total bummer, dudes."

"I can't believe that Verta Mae Sneed was at the center of all this. Sure, Henriette was wrong, but what Verta Mae did was even worse. She was a member of the Invisible 7, and she worked on an exhibit that, according to them, literally rendered them invisible as artists." Alex jumped out of her seat. "I knew from the moment we met her that we couldn't trust her."

Jin wasn't sure. She left the Schomburg feeling more confused than ever. Everything kept shifting, the threads of this increasingly complicated story slipping out of her grasp.

Later that night, an official announcement on the evening news reported that the recently discovered painting, the one she'd illegally photographed earlier, had conclusively been determined to be the work of Henriette Drummond. *That must've been why Markum and all the reporters were at the hospital,* Jin thought. The camera cut to a woman with stringy hair, who was a professor of art at some university. "The discovery of this painting may certainly have a significant impact on the cultural and economic future of Harlem," the woman said.

The future. The words jumped out at her. She thought about the murals and about the controversy over the *Harlem on My Mind* exhibit, and suddenly she understood why the paintings were so important. This whole mess was not about fine art at all, it was about control. Whoever controlled the paintings controlled not the only the story, but potentially, the future of Harlem.

Rose called Jin on Saturday, a few days after the visit to the hospital and the Schomburg Center. She had information about the vintage hat they'd found in Elvin's grandfather's apartment. Jin had already agreed to meet Elvin and Alex that afternoon, so she invited Rose to come along.

"Going to study with Rose!" Jin called to Halmoni before leaving the bodega.

Halmoni stopped her and handed her a bag of groceries. "For the boy," she said. "And don't forget, we have big kimchi order to fill tonight. You come home early."

Jin blushed as she headed out the door, embarrassed that Halmoni had caught her in a lie. Well, half a lie. Technically, she was helping Rose with her schoolwork. They'd agreed that Rose could use whatever she found out about the hat in her research project. *Take that, Halmoni!* Jin thought with a satisfied nod.

Rose was already sitting on the front

stoop of her building, the hatbox balanced carefully on her knees, when Jin turned onto her block. As Jin got closer, she could see that the box had been wrapped in several layers of Bubble Wrap and packing tape. "Was that really necessary?" She pointed at the box. "We're only going a few blocks."

Rose looked appalled. "Of course it's necessary. This is haute couture. If I could afford it, I would have hired an armored car to transport something this beautiful and rare." Rose was very serious about fashion.

"Suit yourself." Jin shrugged as Rose bounced along beside her, gingerly cradling the box. After she'd broken the news that Noodles' prospective new home had been partially demolished, Rose had been pretty down. Jin was happy to see that she seemed to be in a good mood today. "How's your history project going?" Jin asked her.

"Fabulously, thanks to this hat. You have no idea what a great find this is. It's perfect for my fashion timeline. Do you think I could take it to school for the final presentation?"

"I'll have to ask Elvin about that."

"I would just love to be able to show an actual item by a famous Harlem designer, who—"

"Stop! Don't tell me anymore. I want us all to

hear about the hat at the same time." Jin covered her ears.

"Fine, but the suspense is killing me!" Rose groaned. "Let's talk about something else. How about *your* history project? How're things with Mystery Girl?"

"Very mysterious," Jin joked. "Seriously, though we've been working on our project, we just haven't done a lot of work, if that makes sense. I mean, we've gathered a lot of good information, but we haven't organized it yet."

"You'd better hurry. Ms. Weir wants an outline and summary of our projects by Monday."

"Thanks for reminding me," Jin said, surprised at how calm she felt. Normally, she was obsessive about assignment due dates. The thought of turning something in late could bring on an instant panic attack. Of course, this could still happen if, come Sunday night, she hadn't finished her assignment, but, for now, at least, she wasn't worried. *Weird.*

Alex was already at Elvin's when they arrived. After letting them in, Alex plopped back down in the armchair where she'd been sitting and put her feet up on the ottoman. Elvin was bent over a pile of papers on the coffee table, frowning with concentration.

"What's he doing?" Jin asked.

"Homework," Alex answered nonchalantly.

Elvin grinned up at them. "I'm doing Alex's homework."

"Alex! How could you?" Jin gasped.

"It was his idea," Alex said.

"It's true. I asked her if she had any homework. I was kind of missing school for some strange reason," Elvin explained.

"Don't you worry, my friend. There's plenty more where that came from." Alex stretched back into the chair, folding her arms behind her head.

"Elvin, this is my friend Rose O'Malley. She has some stuff to tell us about the hat we found at your grandfather's apartment," Jin said.

Elvin put his work aside and Alex drifted over to the couch so they could all gather around the coffee table. Rose placed the box in the center.

"First of all, I want to thank you for the honor and the privilege to research this hat. It's not every day that I encounter an Isabel Drummond-Hernandez original," Rose began.

"Were you able to find out if this Drummond is related to our Henriette Drummond?" Elvin asked.

"I don't know for sure, but it could be," Rose said. "Isabel Drummond-Hernandez was very active in the Harlem art scene, and a very well-known designer back in the sixties. She was famous for her hats, women's dresses, and men's tailored suits. She was also big in the theater. She did costumes for large Broadway productions, even a few movies. Isabel never followed trends. Her style was unique but still classic and time- less, like the feathered hat. It was probably made in the sixties, but looks like it's from the 1920s, and I would totally wear it today. See? Timeless. By the way, can I wear the hat?"

"No way! Hat's evidence," Alex said firmly.

"Anyway," Rose snapped. "Isabel had a pretty short career. She dropped out of the fashion scene in the seventies. That's why her stuff is so valuable because it's rare. But she's still alive, and she lives right here in Harlem. I would give anything to meet her."

"Let's do it!" Alex jumped out of her seat. "Let's go find Isabel. And bring the hat!"

Rose rushed ahead as they neared the building. "This is it!" she called, waving her arms in the air with excite- ment. Alex marched up to her and dragged her off to one side.

"This is an investigation, not a parade," she

admonished. "We're not trying to let the whole neigh-borhood know what we're up to."

"Sorry." Rose wrenched her arm away from Alex. "I'm just excited. We're about to meet a fashion icon. It's not my fault if you can't appreciate that."

"Can we please just go in?" Jin brushed past Rose and Alex to get to the building's entrance. She ran her finger down the list of names beside the buzzers until she found one marked IDH. "This must be it."

"Oh, please let me!" Rose nudged her aside to push the buzzer.

"Who's there?" a frail-sounding woman's voice crackled through the intercom.

"Mrs. Hernandez, my friends and I would like to talk to you about an important matter," Alex spoke up in a professional-sounding manner before Rose could answer.

"Please leave me alone. I don't have what you're looking for," the voice quivered.

"Actually, we have something that might be of interest to you." Rose elbowed her way back to the speaker. "I'm holding in my hands a white 1920s-style feather hat. There are jewels around the rim, I'm guessing emeralds, with a short veil on the front. We just want to ask you a few questions about it. "

"We're all in seventh grade, by the way," Jin added. There was a long pause, before a buzzer sounded to let them in. Rose led the way up the stairs to Isabel's apartment and knocked firmly on the door. A woman opened it, just a crack. Rose held the hat up, and once the woman had gotten a good look at it, she opened the door the rest of the way.

"Do come in." A tall, thin, elderly woman ushered them inside. She wore a stylish black wrap dress and a pair of very large black eyeglasses. Her gray hair was pulled into a neat bun, emphasizing her gleaming, and still youthful-looking olive skin.

"Mrs. Hernandez, I just want to say it is such an honor to meet you. I just feel compelled to hug you," Rose gushed after the introductions had been made.

"Thank you, dear. And please call me Isabel." She led the small group into a large, elegant living room, with a sparkling chandelier and gleaming wood floors. "Please have a seat."

Jin, Alex, Elvin, and Rose all sat on a long, modern-looking couch with a low back.

"Is this an Eames couch?" Rose asked.

"Good eye," the woman said as she sat across from them near the window in an old-fashioned rocking chair that seemed out of place amid the rest of the modern furniture in the room. "I apologize for my rudeness earlier," she sighed. "It's just that I thought you might've been working with *him*."

"With who?" Jin pulled out her notebook.

"I don't know exactly. A young man with big hair has been coming around harassing me. He rings my bell, or bangs on my door, always yelling for me to give back what belongs to him."

"Do you have any idea what he wants?" Jin asked.

"No, but let's not talk about that." Isabel waved her hand. "Please, may I take a closer look at the hat?"

Rose carefully removed it from the box. Isabel's hands flew to her chest.

"I don't believe it. Where did you get this?" She reached for the hat, fingers trembling.

"It was in my grandfather's apartment. His name is Jacob Morrow," Elvin said.

"He kept it." Tears began to streak down Isabel's face as she stroked the hat.

"Do you know my grandfather, Miss Isabel?" Elvin asked, a hopeful look on his face.

Isabel nodded. "I knew him very well. This hat, I made it for your grandmother Theresa to wear on their wedding day. She died so young, too young." She shook her head.

"I know, my mom told me," Elvin said sadly. Jin and Alex shot him a questioning look.

"What's this about a grandmother?" Alex asked.

"I'll tell you later," Elvin said, and turned back to Isabel. He told her the story of his mother being sick, his grandfather's attack, and how they were now on the hunt for valuable missing paintings by an artist named Henriette Drummond. "We think whoever did this to my grandfather wants those paintings."

Isabel studied Elvin for several minutes before speaking. "Henriette Drummond was my sister," she sighed heavily. "No matter how I try to forget, I always feel those days nipping at my heels. I knew that they would catch up with me at some point, and I guess that moment is now. What do you want to know?" She looked at the children expectantly, but they stared back at her with blank expressions. They had anticipated having to pry information out of her, and weren't prepared for the door to the past that she had just flung wide-open.

Jin was the first to speak. "We've, uh, done some research about Henriette, but we still don't understand why she would have destroyed, or possibly hidden her work." Jin swallowed, working up the nerve to ask the next question. "What really happened at

the Metropolitan Museum of Art? With the vandalized paintings?"

Isabel sighed again. "She did it. She confessed to
me in what was to be our last conversation before she
disappeared, though I didn't know it then."

"But why would she do something like that?
Didn't she think that vandalizing paintings belong-
ing to one of the most respected museums in the
world would ruin her career?" Jin exploded.

Isabel patted her hand and smiled. "I think
Henriette honestly felt that it was the right thing to
do. She hated the idea of an elite institution choosing
to depict Harlem and its residents without allowing
those people any say in how they would be repre-
sented. She considered it a crime to steal someone's
story. Maybe vandalizing the paintings was her idea
of payback.

"My sister was always a passionate person. Art was
how she expressed that passion, and she was brilliant
at it. She could've had scholarships to any art school
she wanted, but she helped to found the Invisible 7
instead. You see, Henriette never believed in creating
art for art's sake. She wanted her art to change people's
lives. The six other members of the Invisible 7 were
kindred spirits. Together they found the perfect
balance between art and service to the community."

Isabel paused then and excused herself to get a drink of water. Once she'd left, Rose stood up to wander around the room. "There's so much cool stuff in here," she said as she inspected framed pictures and knickknacks, books, and even furniture. "Look at this ancient stereo console. Do they even make these anymore?" she asked as she ran her hand along the heavy wooden frame, which housed an old-school record player and speakers.

"Will you stop touching stuff?" Alex snapped at her.

"Jin, look!" Rose pointed, ignoring Alex. From the couch, Jin craned her neck to look where Rose was pointing. Two, small pink dog bowls sat on a plastic mat on the floor next to the console. "She has a dog!" Rose squealed.

At that moment, Isabel returned to the room, carrying a tray with five glasses of water.

"What kind of dog do you have?" Rose asked as Isabel handed each of them a glass.

"My GiGi was a Yorkshire Terrier. She died a month ago," Isabel said sadly. Jin and Rose exchanged a knowing glance as Isabel smoothed down her skirt and cleared her throat. "You asked why Henriette would ruin such a promising career." Isabel looked at Jin. "My personal opinion is that she was looking for a way out. It seemed like after she got the fellowship at the Met, her relationship with her work changed. She told me that she didn't feel that her art could have the same meaning or impact caged up in a museum."

"So you think she vandalized the paintings so that she *would* get kicked out of the program?" Alex asked.

"I would like to believe that Henriette was not that selfish a person, that she could not have intended the disastrous consequences that resulted from her decision."

"Like what?" Elvin asked.

"Well, for one, the Invisible 7 disbanded, and all its members, save one, were blacklisted as a bunch of radical extremists. Henriette lost her second commission at Harlem Hospital, and work became hard to come by. It impacted my career as well, and I wasn't even an official member. Once the theaters found out that I was Henriette's sister, the jobs began to dry up. I became a secretary to support myself. Those were very dark days. Many people were badly hurt as a result of Henriette's actions, and those wounds never healed. The people you're looking for may be trying to settle a score," Isabel said, lowering her voice.

"But why go after my grandfather?" Elvin asked. "He's not the one who vandalized the paintings."

"But he was the only one who stood by Henriette. I think Jacob needed the Invisible 7 to distract him from the pain of his wife's death. He was relentless in his attempts to keep the group together. The Goat really earned his nickname." She winked at Elvin.

Elvin's mouth dropped open. "The goat? Seriously?"

"What, he never told you about that?" Isabel laughed. "Henriette always said that Jacob was stubborn as a goat. Then we found out that the goat was the unofficial mascot of Harlem, during the mid- to late-1800s, when this part of New York, still very rural, was home to a large population of goats. The goats created quite a nuisance, as I understand. And since your grandfather was so passionate about Harlem, sometimes to the point of annoyance, the name just stuck."

"Cool," Elvin said, fingering the Pez dispenser in his pocket. *Could his grandfather be trying to tell him something?*

"So maybe because Jacob was the only one of the Invisible 7 who stuck by Henriette, someone thinks that she told him what she did with her paintings," Alex speculated.

"That's possible, but my sister told me that she was planning to destroy all her paintings. Now, Henriette has always been impulsive, so she may have changed her mind, but she expressly said that the mural at the hospital was to be the last of her paintings to be shown publicly."

"Is that why the feather on that painting is black and not green?" Jin asked. "Was she trying to tell everyone that she planned to disappear?"

Isabel cocked her head thoughtfully. "I'm not sure. I always thought of that feather as Henriette's way of apologizing to the Invisible 7 for the darkness she'd brought into their lives."

"What about the painting that was discovered in the community garden? The hospital is claiming that it belongs to them. Was that a sketch for the second commission that she lost after the whole fiasco at the Met?" Jin pressed.

Isabel sucked her teeth. "That's what they want the world to believe, but the piece that was discovered was actually a sketch for Henriette's original idea for the *first* mural. They rejected that idea because Henriette included images of nontraditional healers, which ran contrary to the belief in this country that Western doctors are the only valid medical practitioners. They no more own that sketch than I own that hospital," Isabel spat. She dabbed at the corners of her eyes with a handkerchief that she pulled out of her sleeve, then stood up abruptly. "I have something I'd like to give you."

She walked over to a desk in the corner of the room, and returned with a photograph, which she handed to Elvin. "I don't know if this will help you in your search, but this is a picture of me with the Invisible 7 in happier days. It's only a copy, I'm afraid. There's your grandfather, and that's me and my sister next to him." Isabel lightly touched each of the three, smiling faces. "How young and hopeful we were then. I hope you will think of us and remember us that way," she said, meeting the eyes of each of the four young people in her living room.

"Now, if you will excuse me, children, I need to lie down. Talking about the past has taken a lot out of me." Isabel led them to the foyer. She shook hands with Jin, Alex, and Rose. With Elvin, though, she placed her hands on either side of his face, then hugged him. "Your grandmother would've been so pleased to know you, had she lived. Take care of your grandfather," she whispered as the door shut quietly behind them.

· · ·

The four lingered outside the building for a few minutes, before heading off in separate directions. Elvin was going skateboarding with Rad, Rose had to get home to pack, Alex had to go out with her parents, and Jin was expected back at the bodega.

"Hey, wait a second," Jin called after Alex, who had already started down the block. "We need to talk about our project at some point. We have an outline and summary due on Monday."

Alex seemed fidgety. "Can we do it later? My mom has already texted me like ten times asking where I am."

"Where are you guys going?"

Alex looked down at the sidewalk. "Just some dinner for my dad's job. I don't want to talk about it."

So we're back to being Mystery Girl, Jin thought. "Okay, well, have a good time, I guess."

Alex started to walk away, then suddenly turned back. "Jin, I need to tell you something. I wanted to tell you sooner, but Elvin was so upset that day at the hospital that I didn't think I should bring it up," Alex blurted out in one breath.

"What is it?" Jin sighed.

"Your grandparents' bodega—it's on Markum's list."

"What?"

"It's on the list. Markum is planning to demolish it. I wanted you to know, so that you could be on the lookout for . . ."

Jin felt the blood rush to her ears. She was so angry, she couldn't even hear what Alex was saying. How could Alex have waited to tell her this? Real friends didn't keep secrets. And a real friend would have wanted her to have as much time as possible to warn Halmoni and Harabeoji and fight Markum. Did Alex even consider Jin and Elvin her friends at all? Or were they just her newest charity cases? Jin wasn't sure. "I can't do this anymore," she whispered.

And before Alex could say anything else, Jin was gone.

CHAPTER 18

Jin was so spooked when she got back to the bodega, she could barely concentrate on her chores. Her eyes darted to the door every time someone came in, wondering if they were spies sent by Markum. And when the produce guy delivered two boxes of lettuce crawling with bugs, Jin suspected that it was some kind of threat or warning from Markum. Later, while she was helping Halmoni and Harabeoji pack jars of kimchi for the big order from the Korean Embassy, Jin dropped two jars before Halmoni banished her to the cubby behind the deli counter.

"Jinnie, why so jumpy today?" Halmoni asked as she continued packing.

"No reason." Jin considered telling her about Markum's list, but she didn't want to worry her grandmother, and if Halmoni already knew, she didn't want to make the bad news worse by bringing it up. "Halmoni, why do you hate Councilman Markum so much?"

Halmoni frowned and glanced at Harabeoji at the mention of Markum's name. "No hate, just very, very disappointed. And angry. We have work hard to bring people together in this neighborhood, and Markum work very hard to tear our neighborhood apart."

"What do you mean?" Jin poked her head out from her cubby.

Harabeoji cleared his throat. "Your grandmother and I open our store here many years ago, but it has not always been so easy. We didn't always get along with our neighbors. Sometimes it was like we live on two separate islands, but we spend a lot of time building bridges to connect us." Harabeoji clasped his two hands together. "Markum make people afraid, make them feel they have to fight to protect what they have, and turn away from their neighbor." Harabeoji shook his head sadly, then bent over so that he was eye level with Jin. He clasped his hands again, lacing all the fingers together. "Remember this." He shook his interwoven hands. "This is our strength. As long as we stand together, Markum cannot win."

"I'll remember." Jin interlaced her own fingers, mirroring her grandfather's, and leaned back into her cubby. Tucked away in her secret space, with a cozy pillow to snuggle, and grandparents to protect her from the scary things and people lurking just beyond the deli case, Jin felt safer, calmer. But staring down at her clasped hands, she thought about what Harabeoji had said about unity, and the uneasiness began to creep back up her spine. She had made a terrible mistake today when she told Alex that she was off the case. She had walked out on her friends— yes, she could definitely call them that now—when they needed her most. Jin wasn't sure how, but she had to fix this. She reached for her phone to call Alex, but Alex had already texted her.

> *J—I am so sorry about today. I need to talk to you—about everything. Will you come over tomorrow around noon? I'll text the address later.*

Jin was relieved. Maybe Alex actually did care about their friendship. She texted back: *I'm really sorry, too. I'll be there.*

Alex knew that she'd messed up, big-time. She'd been keeping secrets for so long, she wasn't even sure anymore why she was doing it. At first, she'd done it to protect herself. She had an automatic wall that went up whenever she met someone new. When most kids found out her family had money, they wanted to be her friend because they thought it would bring them a step closer to the rich and famous. Others made a point of ignoring her, letting her know that her money didn't make her any better than them—not that she would've ever thought that. Either way, it was easier to keep her distance than be disappointed that no one really saw her. Jin and Elvin weren't like that, though. They were for real. The least she could do was tell them the truth.

After sending a quick text to Jin, Alex rushed over to the neighborhood library. She'd promised the librarian that she'd deliver some books the library was donating to Harlem Hospital. She'd have to hurry so she could make it home in time to attend that stupid fundraiser with her parents. Arrgh! That was yet another thing she hadn't told Jin and Elvin. The fundraiser was for Councilman Markum's reelection campaign, and it was being held at the Metropolitan Museum of Art. She felt awful for keeping it from them, but she swore to herself that she'd come clean about the whole thing when they met tomorrow.

Alex dropped off the books at the hospital. On her way out, the receptionist with the platinum-blond hair and long pink nails called out to her. "Yoo-hoo! Young lady!"

Alex looked around and then pointed to herself. "Me?" She mouthed the word.

The woman bobbed her head up and down and waved her over to the desk.

"You were the one asking about the old man in the coma the other day. You're his niece, right?" she whispered.

"Er, yeah," Alex nodded, remembering the lie she'd told. The woman leaned toward her. "He's awake. I just updated the status report myself. I was hoping you'd come in."

Alex could've hugged her. Instead, she shook the receptionist's hand until the woman gently tugged it away. "Thank you so much! My friend . . . I mean, my family will be so happy!"

As soon as she was outside, Alex called Elvin, but there was no answer. She left a message. "Elvin, call me ASAP. I have something very important to tell you."

⁖ ⁘ ⁖

Elvin was too busy looking at the photograph that Isabel had given him to notice his cell phone ringing. The photo was clutched tightly in his hand as he entered St. Nicholas Park. He scanned the clusters of skater kids but didn't see Rad among them, so he sat down on an empty bench to study the photograph one more time. He stared into his grandfather's youthful smiling face. In a month's time, he had gone from knowing nothing about his grandfather to being the keeper of his legacy, literally. People kept giving him things to ensure that he would always remember Jacob Morrow. But what exactly was he supposed to remember?

Elvin looked up from the picture and glanced around the park again. He still didn't see Rad anywhere, but he did spot someone familiar. T.J., the graffiti wunderkind Rad had introduced them to the day he, Jin, and Alex broke into his grandfather's apartment, was walking right toward him, his high-top fade even taller than when they first met. Not up for a conversation, Elvin ducked his head down and held the picture up to cover his face until T.J. had passed him. Elvin had thought the guy seemed kind of dangerous when they first met, and now, glancing over the edge of his photo, he saw something that confirmed his suspicion. Shaved into the back of T.J.'s head was a zigzag pattern, like two lightning bolts. *Zig-Zag!* Could T.J. have been the guy that had pushed Jarvis Monroe around?

Elvin had to follow him and find out what he was

up to. He trailed T.J. out of the park and onto St. Nicholas Avenue, headed downtown until they reached 125th Street, where T.J. disappeared into a storefront near the corner. Elvin crept closer to get a look at the front of the building. It was the campaign headquarters of Councilman Geld Markum. *What was T.J. doing here?* Elvin sent a quick text message to Rad letting him know where he was and his suspicions about T.J., then crept inside.

He found himself in a small waiting area, empty except for a desk and a few multicolored plastic chairs. Campaign leaflets were scattered on the desk, but other than that, there was no sign that anyone actually worked here. Elvin heard voices coming from a back room and inched toward the sound. He didn't see anyone, but he was starting to think that maybe it wasn't such a good idea for him to go back there alone. He'd come back with Rad and the girls, Elvin decided, and turned to leave.

Suddenly, he felt a hand clamp down his shoulder. "May I help you, young man? Here to volunteer for the councilman?" A kindly looking older man, tall and lean, with a neatly trimmed salt-and-pepper Afro, grinned down at him. His face was familiar. Elvin's brain snapped into action, even as the rest of his body was frozen with fear.

"No volunteering for me. I can't even vote." Elvin chuckled nervously. "I think I'm in the wrong . . ." His voice trailed off mid-sentence as he realized that he had seen this man—or at least a much younger version of him—in Isabel's photograph. "Um, I was just curious, were you a member of the Invisible 7? We read about the group in school," Elvin said hesitantly. He wasn't sure yet whether this guy was friend or foe.

A smile spread across the man's face. "Why, yes, I was. Nice that they're still teaching the youngbloods about us."

"I love the murals you guys made. We saw some of them. And I heard that a painting was discovered by another one of the Invisible 7, someone named Henriette Drummond. She was like the leader of the Invisible 7, right?"

The man's eyes hardened. "There was no leader," he said in a strained voice. "We all worked equally to promote our mission. Henriette just took all the credit."

Elvin nodded. He knew he should think of something else to say, but what? He let his gaze drop to the floor to buy some time, and that's when he noticed the man's shoes, pointy-toed, olive-colored alligator skin boots. They were the same boots the man at the construction site had been wearing!

"Uh, it was really great to meet you, but I've got to get going." Elvin backed toward the door, sure that whoever this man might be, he was definitely bad news. But just as he turned to leave, the man grasped his shoulder again.

"What's the rush? Stay awhile," the man sneered. He led Elvin toward the back offices and into a windowless room where, sitting around a small table were T.J. and the balding, whiny-voiced man from the museum.

"Gentlemen, we have a guest," the older man said.

The bald man stood up and grabbed Elvin's coat collar. "If it isn't my favorite little spy. Do you think I don't know what you sniveling roaches have been up to? Don't try to look innocent!" Museum Guy tightened his grip. "I overheard every word you and your sidekicks said when you went crying to Verta Mae Sneed at the museum. And then, in your grandfather's little roach motel of an apartment, you had the audacity to kick me in the nose!"

"Yeah, your nose was black and blue for days, wasn't it, Pugnacio?" T.J. cackled.

"Shut up, you imbecile," Pugnacio spat at T.J. Then he turned back to Elvin and gave him a hard shake. "I would return the favor and crush every bone in your pathetic little body, except I need something from you. Tell me where the rest of the paintings are," he growled.

Elvin didn't say anything.

"I get it. You're trying to be courageous like your grandfather," Pugnacio laughed.

"You see how far that got him. Lights out, old man," T.J. snorted.

Elvin's heart stopped. T.J. had basically just admitted to attacking his grandfather. "I don't know where the paintings are." Elvin tried to sound tough, but he couldn't control the tremble in his voice.

The older man stepped up and pushed both T.J. and Pugnacio aside. "I suppose we could've waited for your friend to add the next chapter in her little notebook. Oh, don't look so shocked. We saw you three running from the construction site that day," he chided, and tossed Jin's notebook onto the table. "But we're done playing games now." He leaned toward Elvin, so close, their noses were nearly touching. "Tell us what we want to know," he snarled.

"I don't know anything. I only just met my grandfather a few weeks ago. Why would he tell me something so secret?" Elvin felt a rush of anger rising in his chest. "Besides, those paintings aren't yours anyway."

The older man reared up to his full height. "Those paintings are payback for the life that Henriette stole from me when she decided to pull that stupid vandalism stunt at the Met. Make no mistake, they are more mine than *hers*." He spat the words.

"Uh, sorry to interrupt, boss." T.J. tapped the man on the shoulder. "We need to get going. Markum will be expecting us soon."

"Let's take the kid along as a little insurance policy." Pugnacio moved toward Elvin and grabbed one of his arms, while T.J. attached himself to the other. The older man led the way to a car parked out front.

As soon as the small entourage stepped onto the sidewalk, Elvin heard a voice call out.

"Hey, T.J.! What up, dude?"

Elvin looked up just in time to see Rad charging toward them on his board.

"Yo, homey, stop!" T.J. called, but it was too late. Just when it looked like Rad was about to crash into them, T.J. let go of Elvin and scattered, but Pugnacio held on tight. Thinking fast, Elvin pulled the goat Pez dispenser out of his coat pocket and jabbed the man with it in his soft, fleshy side. Pugnacio yelped and released his grip just enough for Elvin to slip away.

Rad spun back around and slid Elvin his board.

"Go, dude, go!" He took off running, while Elvin skated away in the opposite direction.

Elvin didn't stop until he'd reached the apartment. Safe inside, he collapsed on the couch, shaking with exhaustion, fear, and, yes, excitement. After he'd had a chance to catch his breath, he dialed Rad.

"That was awesome, dude!" Elvin said. "Thanks for saving my life."

"No worries, man. Just bring back my board."

"No problem. Are you good?"

"Safe and secure, back at the Rad pad. Over and out."

When Elvin hung up, he noticed that he had a message from Alex, and called her back. "You'll never guess what happened to me!" he started, but Alex cut him off.

"I can't talk right now, but I have great news. I found out that your grandfather is awake. He came out of the coma. Also, can you come by my house tomorrow? We're meeting around noon." When Elvin agreed, she gave him the address and promptly hung up before he could tell her about his adventures with Pugnacio and T.J.

Elvin quickly went online and looked up the visiting hours for the hospital. They were over for the night. He called the hospital switchboard and got transferred to his grandfather's room, but a nurse answered and told him that his grandfather was resting and could not be disturbed.

Still full of energy, Elvin paced the length of the apartment several times before settling again on the couch. *The Life of the Invisibles* lay on the other end of the couch where he'd tossed it the last time he attempted to figure out the poems. He reached for it, noticing a picture of a goat stamped on the back cover that he hadn't paid attention to before. Was it another message from his grandfather?

Elvin cracked open the book, reading now with all the focus and determination he could muster. But the poems still weren't making sense. It wasn't until he got to one near the middle of the book that something jumped out at him. The poem was short and simple:

Meet me at the Skillet.
They'll surely make us something good to eat.
I won't have far to travel.
I'm just across the street.

He remembered the walking tour they'd gone on with Rad to look at some of the Invisible 7 murals. There had been a mural directly across the street from the Magic Skillet restaurant, just like in the poem. He read the poem a few more times, and slowly, a new possibility suggested itself. Elvin had expended so much energy trying to figure out what the people in the poems were talking about. What if the voices in the poems did not belong to people at all, but to paintings?

Elvin quickly dialed Jin. "Can you meet me early tomorrow, before we go to Alex's? I need your help. I think I figured out how to find the paintings."

CHAPTER 19

Alex really wanted to hear Elvin's news, but her mom was already nagging her to put her phone away, and they hadn't even made it into the fundraiser yet. As they climbed the long flight of stairs to the grand entrance of the Metropolitan Museum of Art, Cassandra tugged at Alex's hair, and at the sunflower-yellow dress she'd forced her daughter to wear.

"You should wear bright colors. They make you look so, so cheerful," Alex's mother beamed.

Alex didn't say anything. It was pointless arguing with her mother. Once they were inside, Alex probably wouldn't see her parents until the end of the night anyway. When it came to parties, it was Roebuck family custom to split up at the coat check at the beginning and meet back there at the end of the evening. As soon as their coats were on racks, Alex's parents floated away in separate directions to chat, schmooze, and work the room, while Alex usually found a corner chair to plant herself in until she got the signal that it was time to leave.

Tonight, though, Alex had plans of her own. She wanted to explore the museum to find out anything she could about Henriette and the paintings, and she didn't want her parents getting in the way. All she had to do was make it to the coat check and she'd be free to roam.

At the top of the steps, a doorman dressed in a cap and a long, ornate coat with shiny gold buttons and tassels on the shoulders ushered them inside. Alex observed that he didn't look at her family or other guests as he held the door open for them. Then her dad slipped the doorman a bill, also not making eye contact. A thought suddenly occurred to her: *Everyone is invisible to someone.* Alex's mom didn't really see her, and neither her dad nor the doorman noticed each other at all. She, too, had hidden part of herself from Jin and Alex. There were so many ways that people were invisible to each other.

After they checked their coats, Alex followed her parents to the fringes of the Great Hall, where they surveyed the festivities.

"I see Peterson over there. I need to talk to him about the financing on this next deal." Alex's father nodded toward the shiny head of a bald man across the room.

"As you wish, Richard. I suppose I should say hello to Barb Sadler, even though I still can't believe she didn't invite me to join the planning committee for the children's hospital charity drive." Cassandra frowned.

Alex's father gave a vague nod, his mind already focused on his target on the other side of the room. "I'll see you ladies later," Richard said, making a beeline for Peterson.

"You going to be okay, honey?" Alex's mother asked, primping Alex's hair once more. "Make sure you eat something." She gestured in the general direction of the food. "See you back here in a couple of hours."

Alex watched her mother glide away. She spent the next hour nibbling on Brie and wondering about the Rembrandt Henriette had defaced with a defiant letter *H* all those years ago. She could understand the spark of raw emotion that had made her lash out. Even if Henriette had done something unforgivable, that kind of passion was admirable. Henriette believed in something. And that was more than Alex could say for most of the people at the fundraiser. They only believed in their stock portfolios and their perfect glossy images.

She'd just about given up on anything interesting happening when she noticed her dad standing with a group of people crowded around a table headed by a recognizable face. As she got closer, she could see that on the table sat a model of the Harlem World development.

"How is it possible that no one has come up with this idea before me, a simple Harlem boy, son of Georgia sharecroppers, trying to make it in the big city?" Councilman Geld Markum asked the group with a booming, jovial laugh. Alex scooted closer to her dad.

"Consider the possibilities, friends," Markum continued, launching into what may as well have been a campaign speech. "Harlem World is the entertainment complex of the future. Think about it. Where else could you attend a jazz concert where Billie Holiday and John Coltrane perform on the same stage? In the Ellingtonia Jazz Pavilion, Harlem World visitors will be able to customize and program their own concerts by selecting from our library of holographic images. Same thing with the new Harlem Art Museum. Visitors will be able to paint their own version of masterworks by great African American artists. With your vote to reelect me, you have the opportunity to make this innovative development a reality. Especially you, Rich." Markum gripped her dad's shoulder like they were old friends. "I'd love to be able to say that Roebuck Development, Harlem's premiere development company, is partnering with me on this."

Alex held her breath. Would her dad really get involved in a project that would cause people to lose their businesses?

"We'll see, Councilman. Let's just get you reelected first. Have you met my daughter, Alexandra?" Richard smiled sheepishly, turning toward Alex.

A dark cloud passed over Markum's face, but he quickly began to smile again. "The pleasure is all mine," he said with a slight bow. "Rich, if I can't get you to sign on the dotted line, will you at least honor me with a photograph with your lovely daughter?"

Before she knew it, Markum and her father were standing on either side of her, and a man with a camera was counting three. A light flashed in her face. By the time the dark splotches faded away, Alex's dad had already vanished to talk to someone else. And the councilman had moved on to a tall, thin woman with a beak nose and impossibly flat hair on the other side of the model. It was Verta Mae Sneed.

Neither Markum nor Dr. Sneed were looking in her direction. Alex quickly ducked beneath the table so she could listen unseen.

"You and I both know, Councilman, that this Harlem World project would be an atomic bomb," Verta Mae Sneed was saying. She sounded angry, very angry. "You would destroy businesses, homes, people's livelihoods, not to mention make a mockery of a long and beautiful history of Harlem's arts and culture."

"That's where you're wrong, Dr. Sneed. I, too, want to celebrate our history. I believe Harlem World will do just that."

"History can't be preserved by being turned into an amusement park ride."

"History dies if it doesn't get passed on. This is a new day. We've got to reach out to the people where they are. The Board of Directors at your beloved Studio Museum are certainly excited about the new possibilities that Harlem World will bring. Open your mind, Dr. Sneed. Move with the tide, or risk being washed away."

"I assure you, I will do everything within my power to stop this project," Verta Mae spat. Alex heard footsteps and lifted the tablecloth just a smidge in time to see the heels of Verta Mae's shoes as she stormed away. Markum walked off in the opposite direction. *So Verta Mae isn't working with Markum,* Alex noted.

When the coast was clear, she crawled out from underneath the table. She took out her phone to text

Jin and Elvin this new tidbit of information, but the screen promptly fizzled to black. Arrgh! Her phone was out of power, and she didn't have her charger. *Now what?* Thankfully, it was almost time to meet her parents. She would be home soon and would text her friends then.

Heading toward the coat check, Alex glimpsed two men huddled in deep conversation on the outskirts of the party near the membership desk. One of them was Councilman Markum. The other man, short and round with a pudgy moon face, also looked familiar. Alex squinted. It was the man Elvin had seen that night at the museum, the same one who had tried to kill all three of them with a wrecking ball. It had already been quite an adventurous evening, but Alex had to find out what they were talking about. She wove her way through the crowd, ducking behind waiters and unsuspecting guests, until she arrived at the desk and slid behind it.

"Any word on the paintings?" Markum was asking the man. "They are the lynchpin of this entire development. Being able to showcase the missing paintings of a talented, yet conveniently controversial artist like Henriette Drummond will give the development historical legitimacy. As the founder of the

Invisible whatevers, she's a perfect symbol for community activists and artists alike. Displaying her work provides a veneer of authenticity and relevance that the project desperately needs. If those paintings are out there, we've got to have them. You won't let me down on this one, will you, Pugnacio?" Markum sneered at the man.

"Oh, no, sir," Pugnacio said in his sniveling, whiny voice.

"That's what I want to hear. You deliver the goods, and you will helm Harlem World's new art museum."

"And my father? You'll find some ceremonial role for him, won't you?" Pugnacio asked. "He's had his heart set on running the new museum, but we both know he's a bit long in the tooth for the day-to-day operation of such an important institution."

"Not to worry, my friend. Your father will be taken care of. But you are just the kind of forward-thinking person we need to lead the museum toward entertainment and profit. One who appreciates the value of collaboration," Markum said, then paused. "Er, there's just one other small matter. Dr. Sneed is really becoming a thorn in my side. Any way you could, uh, handle that?"

"Leave her to me," Pugnacio wheezed.

"Very well. Good evening, Mr. Green," Markum said, before Alex heard footsteps hurrying away.

Pugnacio Green! Alex found a pen on top of the desk and quickly wrote the name on her hand. She peeked out from behind the desk. Pugnacio was headed toward the Egyptian art galleries. Alex followed—she couldn't give up now, not when things were getting so interesting.

Pugnacio Green walked briskly through the Egyptian wing and into the room that housed the Temple of Dendur, which, Alex remembered from a class trip, honored the goddess Isis. Alex crouched near the entrance of the room, and peeked inside. Clustered in front of the temple were Pugnacio, Rad's friend T.J., and a tall, thin, older man with an Afro. The men spoke in hushed tones. From her perch, Alex strained to hear what they were saying.

"Did you talk to him?" the old man asked. He wrung his hands and paced back and forth in front of the temple.

"Yeah, Pop. I spoke to him," Pugnacio snipped.

Pop? Alex hoped she could remember all this stuff to tell Jin and Elvin.

"And you told him the deal? That if we deliver the paintings, I get to run the new Harlem World museum?" The older man stopped pacing to look at Pugnacio.

"Yes, of course," Pugnacio said quickly.

"And don't forget about me," T.J. piped up. "Markum agreed to give me my own gallery show, right? I just had another idea for an exhibit. What if we invented special markers that made hip-hop beats when you drew with them? That way, people could create their own tag and beats to go with it, kind of like a soundtrack. Dope, right?"

"Yes, yes, brilliant. I'm sure Markum will be open to that." Pugnacio waved his hand in front of his face, as if he were swatting a fly.

So that's the game, Alex thought to herself. Pugnacio Green was playing both sides, willing to sell out his own father. She leaned against a rack of museum pamphlets while she took a few more notes on her hand. Suddenly, the rack shifted a couple inches beneath her weight, loudly scraping the floor. Surprised by the sudden movement, Alex lost her balance and tumbled. As she scrambled to get up, she felt a pair of arms grab her from behind. "Where you going, nosy girl?"

Alex struggled as T.J. dragged her into the temple room.

"You children certainly are tenacious." Pugnacio tsked. "Makes me quite ill."

"Whaddya want me to do with her, boss?" T.J. asked, struggling to hold Alex, who was fighting to get away.

As Pugnacio looked around the room for a suitable place to restrain her, Alex had an idea. She stopped fighting for a moment and stood still.

"See, you tired yourself out," T.J. said. Alex glanced down at T.J.'s high-top sneakers and estimated where his shin might be. She took a deep breath, lifted her leg, and kicked backward as hard as she could. Her pointed kitten heel made direct contact.

T.J. yelped and let her go. Alex took off running and made it out of the gallery, the three men close behind her. Back in the corridor, she noticed an entrance leading to the next gallery and sprinted toward it.

"She's headed for the American Wing!" Alex heard one of the men shout. She glanced over her shoulder. The old man was doubled over, but T.J. and Pugnacio were gaining on her. She picked up speed and wove her way through the American Wing to the Arms and Armor gallery. She ducked behind a statue, which featured a group of knights on horseback, to catch her breath. She could hear T.J. and Pugnacio approaching.

"Where'd she go?" Pugnacio wheezed at the entrance, just a few feet away. Alex held her breath. Suddenly, she heard someone stomping toward her from the opposite direction. Alex squeezed her eyes shut. *Just let me live, just let me live,* she sent a prayer out to the universe. When she opened her eyes, she was looking at the freshly shined shoes of a museum security guard.

"What are you doing here? These galleries are closed," the guard said sternly.

Alex breathed a sigh of relief. "Sorry, I just got lost."

"Come with me," the guard led her out of the gallery. Pugnacio and T.J. were nowhere in sight.

For once, Alex was happy to see her parents, but they, on the other hand, were mortified to have a security guard deliver their daughter to them.

"How could you embarrass us like this," Cassandra whispered through her teeth, as she rushed Alex into her coat, while her dad did a little damage control.

"Kids will be kids." Richard shrugged, grinning

broadly at the small crowd of couples that had gathered around them. "Good night all," he said with a
wave, and ushered his family out the door to their
waiting car. Neither of Alex's parents asked her how
she was, or where she had been.

Halmoni shook Jin awake early the next morning. "Your friend famous! That strange girl with the crazy hair and shopping cart—I thought she poor, but she famous!" She rattled a newspaper in Jin's face.

Bleary-eyed, Jin squinted at the article and bolted upright. Staring back at her from the grainy photograph was an elegant young woman, standing between two smiling men shaking hands. The girl looked nothing like the Alex she knew, with her expensive dress and fashionable hairstyle. It was only the scowl on the girl's face that gave her away—that was all Alex. Jin couldn't believe what she was seeing. She read the headline above the photo: *"*In Bid for Reelection, Councilman Markum Courts Roebuck Development for Harlem World Project." Then she glanced at the caption: *Councilman Markum pictured here with Richard Roebuck, Principal, Roebuck Development, and his daughter, Alexandra Roebuck.*

"Roebuck very big-time. Construct big buildings downtown, and even here in Harlem. You friend must be very, very rich." Halmoni pointed at the photo over Jin's shoulder.

Jin reached for her phone and typed *Roebuck Development*. She quickly learned that Alex's dad's company was one of the top development firms in the country. They even had offices in London, Sydney, and Hong Kong. How could Alex have kept such a secret? Jin felt anger percolating in her toes. Then, like water boiling, her fury grew hotter and more active as it worked its way through her body. She threw the newspaper on the floor.

"What the matter, Jinnie?" Halmoni asked with a concerned frown.

Jin jumped up. "Alex has been lying to me all along. She refused to tell me anything about her family. Now I find out her dad may be part of a project that could put you out of business." She stormed back and forth across the room.

Halmoni stepped out and blocked her path, placing her hands on either side of Jin's face. "Jinnie, wait a moment. You don't know full story. Why Alex do this? You must find out before making conclusion. As for our business, that not Alex's fault. You can't blame the daughter for the choices of the father," she said gently.

Logically, what Halmoni said made sense, but

even with her grandmother's cool palms on her cheeks, Jin still couldn't calm the angry heat flaring inside her. She felt betrayed by Alex all over again.

After breakfast, which Jin was still too upset to eat, she grabbed the newspaper and told Halmoni she was leaving. She couldn't wait to tell Elvin about Alex's big secret.

When she got to Elvin's apartment, he flung open the door, and she promptly forgot about Alex when she heard his news.

"My grandfather's awake!" Elvin did a jerky dance step around the apartment, pointing his finger up in the air like John Travolta in the classic movie *Saturday Night Fever.*

"That's awesome, Elvin! Have you spoken to him?" Jin asked. Now was definitely not the time to tell him about Alex.

Elvin shook his head. "No, but I was hoping we could go to the hospital before we head to Alex's place," he said, already tugging on his coat.

At the hospital, Jin grabbed Elvin's arm. "If anybody asks you any questions about where you're staying while your grandfather recovers, tell them you're staying with me and my grandparents," she said, certain that Halmoni wouldn't mind.

"Thanks, Jin." Elvin grinned.

"Maybe I should wait outside," Jin said as they stepped off the elevator on Elvin's grandfather's floor, suddenly feeling a little nervous to meet the man she'd learned so much about over the past few weeks.

"No, I want you to meet him," Elvin insisted, and dragged her into the room.

Jacob Morrow sat upright in bed, looking as though he'd just woken up from a short nap, rather than a coma. "Elvin," he said, and opened his arms wide.

Elvin ran to him, and the two shared a long, tearful hug. Jin hung back near the door, until Elvin, wiping his eyes, called her over.

"I made a couple friends while you were asleep. They've been helping me to figure out what happened to you. This is Jin. You'll meet Alex later," Elvin said.

Jacob squinted at her. "From the bodega, right? I know your grandparents from the neighborhood. We go back a long way." He opened his arms, and Jin leaned in for an awkward hug. "Thank you for taking care of my grandson."

"No problem." Jin blushed. "Now, I really am going to wait outside and give you two some privacy."

She slipped out the door, softly pulling it closed behind her.

Jin hung out in the hallway and started on her history homework. An outline and summary of their project was due the next day, and Jin felt a fresh wave of annoyance that Alex wasn't there to help.

Close to noon, Jin knocked and cracked open the door. Elvin had pulled his chair next to Jacob, his elbows resting on the bed. "It's time for our meeting with Alex," she told him.

Elvin looked disappointed to have to leave. "I'll be back tomorrow," he promised. He stood up and walked toward the door. "But before we go, I have one more question. Why were you at the community garden that night?"

Jacob sighed. "A few days before the attack, I'd seen a bunch of people hanging out who'd never been there before. It was like they were looking for something. I thought I should keep an extra eye out, so even though the garden is one of the stops on my regular neighborhood patrol route, I decided to swing by a second time that night."

Jin tapped her chin. "I just remembered something those guys said at the construction site. The garden was on Markum's list. He wanted to demolish it to make room for Harlem World. No one knew about the painting until Jarvis discovered it," she said.

"Did you know it was there?" Elvin asked his grandfather.

Jacob looked away. "Yes, I knew," he sighed. "I thought that whoever was canvassing the garden knew, too. That's why I got you the goat. This neighborhood means something to people, and I wanted it to mean something to you, too. We're a stubborn bunch here, but we protect the things we love. I thought once we got to know each other a little better, I'd show you all the treasures Harlem has to offer. But I'm not so sure that's such a good idea anymore."

Elvin felt confused. He wasn't certain what his grandfather was telling him. "So are there more of Henriette's paintings? And can you help us find them?" he asked.

Jacob shook his head. "After I was attacked, the last thoughts I had before I lost consciousness were of you and your mother. Now that I have a second chance, I want to make amends. I want to make a home and a family for the both of you. Promise me that you'll let this whole business with the paintings go, Elvin. It's too dangerous."

"I really like it here, too. And I'll be careful," was

all Elvin said. He reached into his grandfather's coat pocket and touched the *Invisibles* paperback that he'd brought along to show Jin and Alex what he'd discovered about the poems inside. Suddenly, all the pieces clicked. How had he not figured it out sooner? All the goat references, his grandfather's nickname, the goat on the back cover. His grandfather had written it! He was the author of *The Life of the Invisibles*. "Besides"— Elvin winked at his grandfather—"I have a really great guide."

Jacob sighed and nodded. "My coat looks good on you," he said as Elvin and Jin slipped out the door.

"I'm so glad your grandfather's okay," Jin said once they were outside the hospital and on their way to Alex's. "Did he say when he was coming home?"

"He doesn't know yet, but I hope it's soon. I'm looking forward to getting to know him. He's a pretty cool guy," Elvin said. His feelings about his grandfather were all over the place, like a messy room in his brain. He didn't know what to think about all the secrets his mother had kept about the past, or what their family might be like in the future, now that he'd connected with his grandfather. He was going to need some time to sort everything out—after they found the paintings.

"So who's your guide to Harlem?" Jin asked as they walked. "Rad?"

"Not who. What. I just figured out my grandfather wrote that book Dr. Whitmore gave me. But I'll wait to talk about it until we're all together."

"*The Life of the Invisibles?* Are you serious? Did he just come out and tell you that he wrote it?" Jin asked, impressed.

"It doesn't seem like anyone in my family comes right out and says anything," Elvin said. "But I'm pretty sure I'm right."

Alex's family lived only a few blocks away in a stately four-story brownstone on a small street, overlooking Marcus Garvey Park.

"Nice house." Elvin whistled, starting up the stairs. Jin grabbed his arm.

"Before we go in, there's something you should see." She showed him the newspaper article about Alex's dad and Councilman Markum.

Elvin glanced at it quickly, but then did a double take. "Whoa, is that Alex? She looks like . . . she looks like *a girl?*"

"Ahem. Girls look all kinds of ways."

"But she looks really . . . *pretty*." Elvin still couldn't believe Alex's transformation.

"That's not the point!" Jin said louder than she meant to. "The point is Alex lied to us! How can someone just conveniently never mention that their dad is some multigazillionaire developer?"

"She didn't exactly lie . . ."

"Yeah, she did! Take your apartment, for example. She told us that her dad worked for the company that owned the building, but *he* actually owns the building and the entire company!"

Elvin shrugged. "Maybe she just didn't want to make a big deal out of it."

"You *would* take her side."

"I'm not taking—"

"Come on, we're late," Jin cut him off, and marched up the steps to the front door.

When she pressed the doorbell, she could hear the sound of the chimes echoing through the building.

"Must be huge," Elvin speculated. Jin didn't say anything. A few seconds later, a woman wearing tailored black pants and a cream-colored cashmere sweater, and carrying an iPad answered the door.

"Yes?" She looked at them suspiciously.

"Are you Alex's mom?" Elvin asked.

"No, I'm Mrs. Bennett, the Roebuck house man-ager." She swiped her tablet. "Ah, yes. You must be Miss Roebuck's twelve o'clock. I'll inform her of your arrival." She ushered them inside, just as Alex came rushing down the stairs.

"Hey, guys!" she said.

"Hey," Elvin answered. Jin just nodded curtly.

"Welcome to *mi casa*. Let's sit in the dining room." Alex led them into a large room with a long wooden table, big enough to seat at least twenty people. Alex pressed a button on a nearby wall, and then began speaking directly into the wall.

"We're ready, chef," she said, and turned to Elvin and Jin. "I'm not totally crazy; the intercom's built into the wall," she explained as she plopped into a cushioned chair at one end of the table. "I asked the chef to make us some of his famous chocolate chip cookies. You're going to love them. Have a seat." Elvin slid into the chair beside her, but Jin remained standing.

"I won't be staying long," she said.

A worried look crept across Alex's face. "Why? What's up?"

"Don't you know? Or is that a secret, too?" Jin tossed the newspaper on the table. Alex sighed.

"This wasn't how I wanted it to come out, but I

guess, in some ways, it's a good thing that article was published. I invited you two here so that I could finally tell you—well, show you—who I really am."

"It's a little late for that, don't you think?" Jin rolled her eyes, then sighed. "I hate secrets. Secrets mean you never really know a person; you never know the whole truth about them. They're always going to be hiding something."

"Yeah, secrets suck," Elvin agreed. "They kept me from my grandfather for pretty much my whole life."

"Maybe this wasn't such a good idea," Jin said, and started toward the door.

"You're leaving?" Alex ran after her. "You're seriously walking out again?"

"I don't want to be friends with someone I can't trust," Jin said. "Why do you pretend to be something you're not? I mean, the way that you dress, the donated food, nobody would ever know who you really are. So why do you do it?"

"That's the thing. I'm not pretending," Alex tried to explain. "I am being who I am. That girl in the newspaper, that's the pretend girl. I hate what my parents stand for. You read the article. Councilman Markum is a sleazeball, and even though my dad hasn't agreed to work with him on the Harlem World project yet, that doesn't mean that he won't. He's done other projects that have caused people to lose their homes and their jobs. That's why I volunteer and try to get people to donate to the needy. It may not be much, but I want to do what I can to help people, not make money off their misery. I guess I dress the way I do so that I can be invisible to the wrong people, like my parents and their friends, but visible to the people who matter, like my friends, who I hope can see the real me. I'm really sorry I didn't tell you the truth right away. I wanted to wait for the right time. But you can't just leave. What about Elvin? If it'll make you feel better, *I'll* stop trying to find the paintings."

"No, *I'll* leave!" Elvin shouted. Jin and Alex whirled around to face him. "You guys just don't get it. I'm the one whose family was attacked. I'm the one who's been on my own in a strange city. This is my life, not some stupid game."

"I'm sorry, Elvin. That was really awful of me," Jin apologized.

"Me too, Elvin." Alex's eyes fell to the floor.

"It doesn't matter now, anyway. My grandfather's awake and getting stronger. We pretty much know who attacked him. There's no point in continuing this thing. As soon as my mom gets well enough, I'll be going back to California."

"California?" Alex's head snapped up. "What about the paintings?"

"Maybe my grandfather was right. We should forget about the paintings. Let the past stay in the past."

The words were sharp tiny pinpricks, which made Jin's heart deflate like a balloon slowly losing air. "But this isn't just about us anymore," she said, ashamed now of her own selfishness.

"Yeah, we owe it to the people of Harlem to see this thing through. We can't let Markum get his hands on those paintings. If he does, his project is sure to be approved and it'll destroy the entire community," Alex added.

Elvin ran his hands through his deadlocks. "You're right," he said. "And we owe it to the Invisible 7, too. And to my grandfather."

"We'll finish what we started, right?" Alex said, determined. She looked from Jin to Elvin, who both nodded in agreement.

They wandered back into the dining room and sat down at the table, where the chef had set out a huge plate of warm chocolate chip cookies, and milk served in fancy crystal goblets.

After inhaling a few cookies, Jin took out her notebook. "So this might be a good time to catch up. A lot has happened since we last met up. Who wants to go first?"

"I will!" Elvin volunteered. "Yesterday, when I went to the park, I saw T.J. and realized he was the guy who messed with Jarvis Monroe, so I decided to follow him. He went to Councilman Markum's campaign office. Turns out he's working with Markum, Museum Guy, whose name is Pugnacio, by the way, and this man." He took out the photo that Isabel had given him and pointed to the old man with the salt-and-pepper Afro and fancy boots. "He's also the person who was with Pugnacio at the construction site. He says that when Henriette vandalized those paintings she pretty much ruined his life. Seems like he wants them as some kind of payback."

Next Jin turned to Alex, who was pacing around the table.

"Last night, my parents dragged me to a fund-raiser for Markum. Sorry I didn't tell you guys, but that's my last secret—I promise. Anyway, I overheard a conversation between Markum and none other than our good friend, Verta Mae Sneed. Contrary to popular opinion, Dr. Sneed is not working with Markum.

In fact, she vowed to do everything she could to shut down his whole Harlem World operation."

"That still doesn't rule out the possibility that she wants the paintings for herself," Elvin added.

"True." Alex nodded and continued. "Later, I overheard Markum talking to Pugnacio—this guy really gets around. Pugnacio definitely wants to find the paintings because Markum has promised him a really cushy job as head of the new art museum in Harlem World if he turns them over to him."

"And if their art museum opens, it'll likely replace the Studio Museum and put Verta Mae out of a job," Jin noted. "But why does Markum want the paintings so badly anyway?"

"To make Harlem World more legit. If he can promise to display the long-lost treasures of a Harlem great, his project will get the green light for sure." Alex rolled her eyes and continued. "T.J. and that old man from the construction site were both there, too. Turns out, in addition to being a member of the Invisible 7, the old guy is also Pugnacio's dad, and he thinks that if they find the paintings Markum is going to make *him* the head of the Harlem World art museum. And T.J. thinks that Markum will give him his own graffiti gallery."

"So Pugnacio is playing his own father. That's low," Jin said.

"But not as low as what Markum has planned for Dr. Sneed. He not only wants her gone from the museum, I think he wants her gone, period. Pugnacio said that he would 'handle it.' What if they hurt her? We need to go and warn her," Alex said, glancing at her phone. "And we can still make it to the museum before it closes."

When they got to the Studio Museum, Alex, Jin, and Elvin marched right past the lobby receptionist straight to Dr. Sneed's office. She was sitting behind her huge desk but jumped to her feet when they entered the room. "I take it by your presence here today that you have decided to continue the pursuit for the paintings, against my earlier warnings and advice," Verta Mae said, fixing them in her pitiless gaze.

Undeterred, Alex marched right up to the desk. "You're right, and we've got a lot of questions. We expect you to give us some answers," she demanded.

"I have nothing more to say on the matter." Verta Mae pursed her lips. "I suggest you leave my office now, before I call security."

Jin, Alex, and Elvin exchanged glances, but held their ground.

"Very well." Verta Mae reached for the phone.

"You're in danger! We're here to warn you," Jin blurted out.

After pausing for a beat, Verta Mae

calmly withdrew her hand from the phone and sat down. Alex, Jin, and Elvin sat then, too, in the chairs opposite her desk.

Alex leaned forward. "Now that we have your attention, we need to know—are you or are you not after the paintings? Maybe you want to make a little profit off of them yourself?" she prodded.

"Of course not! I—I only want what's best for the art and for Harlem." For once, Verta Mae seemed flustered.

"I'm not sure that Henriette Drummond would agree, especially since you practically sold her and the entire Invisible 7 out after the exhibit at the Met." Alex leaned back confidently in her chair.

"Henriette was wrong!" Verta Mae shouted. "And I—I—" Verta Mae stopped to collect herself. "Why. are you here? What is it that you want exactly?" she asked icily.

Jin took out her notebook. "We want the truth."

"Yeah, starting with your relationship with the three guys who've been trying to kill us," Elvin piped up. "Are you working with them? Did you set us up?"

Verta Mae raised her eyebrows. "And which three guys would this be?"

"Your coworker, Pugnacio Green, a graffiti artist named, T.J., and this man." Elvin pulled out Isabel's photograph of the Invisible 7 and pointed to the older man he and Alex had seen with Pugnacio. "Who is this?"

Verta Mae shook her head sadly. "I know all of them. And no, we are certainly not in cahoots. The man you pointed to is Clarence Aubrey. I was hoping that he would've healed and moved on, but it looks as though he's still holding on to the hurt he felt all those years ago," she sighed. "Clarence was one of the younger members of the Invisible 7. He started hanging out with us when he was still in high school. He was a talented enough painter but certainly not a prodigy like Henriette. What he lacked in talent, he made up for in his passion for the arts. He eventually became an excellent arts administrator, but he'd had his heart set on being an artist.

"Clarence graduated from high school the spring before the *Harlem on My Mind* exhibit went up at the Met. I presume you've already done your research on the exhibit." Verta Mae paused to look over the rim of her tiny glasses at them. Elvin, Jin, and Alex nodded, and she continued. "When the news about the vandalized paintings at the Met broke, Clarence started receiving rejection letters from all the art schools and internships he'd applied to. And he placed the blame squarely on Henriette and the Invisible 7.

"It was tough for all the members of the Invisible 7, though I admit I was luckier than the others. None of them could find work. Nobody wanted to risk hiring a radical. But I'm not convinced that the fallout from the exhibition was Clarence's main problem. His work needed a bit more time to develop. I encouraged him to focus on creating a few really strong pieces to bolster his portfolio, and to reapply to the various programs in a year or so.

"But Clarence refused to let go of this idea that Henriette had ruined his life. It was a tiny ember of rage burning in his heart, which he's continued to tend all this time. I'm not surprised that he's been seduced by a trickster like Markum who, with all his paper-thin promises and false hopes, has added fuel to Clarence's fire. At this point, I wouldn't be surprised by anything Clarence is willing to do for a chance to get back at Henriette and redeem the life he feels he's lost."

Elvin leaned forward. "What about Pugnacio and T.J.? How do they fit into the picture?"

"Both of them are self-serving, conniving opportunists," Verta Mae said sharply. "As you may know, Pugnacio is Clarence's adopted son. I hired Pugnacio as an administrative assistant here at the museum as a favor to Clarence, and I've regretted it every day since.

Pugnacio is after my job, even though he doesn't have the sense to fill a thimble, or even much of an interest in the arts. No, his passion is power, at any cost. And T.J. is Pugnacio's supposed protégé, a kid he plucked from the streets. He claims to want to expose him to more opportunities and a better way of life, but really, I think Pugnacio keeps T.J. around to do his dirty work."

Alex shook her head. "Like Jin said earlier, we actually came here to tell you that Pugnacio, Clarence, and T.J. are planning something. You're in danger."

Verta Mae sighed. "In my life, the line between friend and enemy has often been blurry. For that, I must accept the lion's share of blame. The choices I've made have not always made me the most popular person."

"The *Harlem on My Mind* exhibit," Jin said as threads of the story began to weave together in her mind like a tapestry. "You were working at the Met when Henriette vandalized those paintings and you were a member of the Invisible 7—why didn't you stand up for your friends? Why didn't you defend them when you knew they weren't the troublemakers and criminals that people thought they were? Why didn't you tell the truth about the Invisible 7?" she challenged.

Verta Mae grimaced. "It was because of me, and my pleading with the museum's board not to press charges that Henriette wasn't arrested and taken to jail. I got Clarence a job with the Cultural Affairs department of New York City, and I slipped Jacob Morrow's poetry to the publisher of an independent press here in Harlem. But you're absolutely right, young lady. When it came down to it, I did not go out on a limb for the Invisible 7. Though I have some regrets about that now, I chose then, and will continue to choose to save myself." Verta Mae locked eyes with each of them from across her desk. "And I suggest that you three choose to do the same."

Alex stood up abruptly. "I think our work here is done. You're no better than the rest of them. Everyone's just out for themselves."

As they headed toward the door, Verta Mae called, "It wasn't all for naught, you know." The three stopped and turned to listen. "As a result of all the protests and heated debate surrounding *Harlem on My Mind*, neighborhood artists were inspired to create institutions that would celebrate and exhibit their work in a way that respected their voices. I was one of the founders of this museum that you're standing in at this very moment. People have their own ways of accomplishing very similar goals. Remember, things are not always as they seem. Eventually, every invisible thing becomes visible."

With that, the three headed out of Verta Mae's office, and immediately began to compare notes about what they had just heard. They were so engrossed in their discussion that they didn't hear the soft padding of a pair of high-top sneakers treading behind them.

"Even when she's trying to be helpful, that Verta Mae Sneed still gives me the creeps," Alex proclaimed once they had left the stillness of the museum, and found a concrete bench outside to sit on.

"Yeah, especially that part at the end when she said, 'Every invisible thing eventually becomes visible.' What was that about?" Jin asked.

Elvin's ears perked up. "That reminds me of what I wanted to tell you guys about the *Invisibles* book. I think it will help us find the paintings." He pulled *The Life of the Invisibles* out of his coat pocket. "I've been reading through this book ever since Dr. Whitmore gave it to me, but I could never figure out what the poems meant. Whenever I have a problem, my mom always tells me to shift the perspective, to try another angle, another way of thinking about it. So yesterday, I tried doing that and I came up with an idea. The title of the book is *The Life of the Invisibles,* right? I started to think, what if it's not the poet or the people who are invisible, but the paintings?"

"That makes sense in a lot of ways," Jin interjected. "Even though the murals by the Invisible 7 are technically visible, they kind of fade into the landscape. Sometimes they even get destroyed like the properties on Markum's list, so that nobody sees them anymore. People forget about the paintings, and they also forget about what was in the painting—the events, the places, and even their neighbors."

"Exactly!" Elvin said. "And if the book is about the 'lives' of the paintings, then wouldn't the poems in the book be a way for them to tell their own stories?"

"Just to be clear, are you saying that the poems are written from the perspective of the paintings?" Alex looked confused.

Elvin bobbed his head up and down excitedly. "I think that through the poems, the paintings are asking us to remember them, to notice them. They *want* us to see them. Take this poem as an example." Elvin opened the book to the poem about the Magic Skillet and read it aloud. "'Meet me at the Skillet/They'll surely make us something good to eat/I won't have far to travel/I'm just across the street.' Get it? That's where the mural that Rad showed us is—*across the street* from the Magic Skillet," he pointed out.

"So in order to find Henriette's missing paintings, maybe we just have to follow the right poems," Alex said, catching on.

"I think so," Elvin said hesitantly. "I haven't exactly tested the theory out."

Jin reached for the book and began flipping through it. "Listen to this," she read. " 'In a writer's garden/a place of quiet repose/alongside the flowers, creativity grows.' Hmm," Jin thought for a minute. "The community garden where the painting was found—it's named after the writer Zora Neale Hurston. And repose, that means to rest or relax."

"Like on a bench," Alex added.

"Exactly! And the part about creativity growing alongside the flowers . . . Flowers grow up from the ground. Remember, Jarvis found the painting buried in the ground next to a bench. It's a little bit of a stretch, but it could make sense," Jin mused. "Let's try out a few more," she suggested.

They continued working through the poems in the book until they had identified most of the murals that they had seen on Rad's walking tour.

"I think this one is about the hospital mural," Jin

said, and read the poem at the end of the book to Alex and Elvin.

"Isabel told us that the hospital mural was Henriette's last known painting, but there's one more poem after it." Alex flipped over the last page.

> *Perched above the door,*
> *In a place horses once called home,*
> *The Harlem Goat now stands watch*
> *Over these four walls that contain both*
> *The beginning and the end.*
> *Tug his beard and he will*
> *Give you the key*
> *To unlock the chamber*
> *Where once there was*
> *Peace without distinction, unity within difference.*
> *Encased in this place, my heart still beats,*
> *Faint as an ember,*
> *A tiny seed,*
> *A dream to be uncovered.*
> *Remember, remember.*

"A place horses once called home, goat perched above the door," Elvin thought aloud. "I remember where I've seen that before. When we were on the mural tour, Rad took us to that abandoned church building that used to be the headquarters of the Invisible 7. He told us that it was originally a stable, so that could be our horses' home. And wasn't there a stone goat head above the door?"

"Sounds like that could be it," Alex suggested. "Let's check it out."

CHAPTER 22

They hopped in a cab and headed for the small brick building on 122nd Street. As the car stopped and started in the heavy traffic, Elvin's stomach began to churn. He rolled down the window and stuck his head outside. The day was brisk but sunny, and he should have felt exhilarated to be finally closing in on the missing paintings, but he couldn't shake the feeling that they were being watched. Even the prickling hairs on his arms thought so.

When the cab finally pulled up to the curb, Alex shot out and pointed to a small stone carving above the stable door. "There's our goat!" She jumped up to try to touch it, but it was too high. "How're we going to tug its beard?"

Jin glanced around and spotted a bodega a few doors down. "I'll be right back." A few minutes later, she returned carrying two empty plastic milk crates. "We always have these lying around our store. One of us should be able to climb on them to reach."

"I'll do it. I'm the tallest in my boots," Alex volunteered.

When the sidewalk was relatively clear and they were sure there were no police in sight, Jin and Elvin stacked the crates and held them steady while Alex climbed on top. The crates gave her just enough height to reach the tip of the goat's beard. She tugged it, waited, and tugged again. "Is this goat supposed to start talking or something, 'cause I'm getting nothing here. What does the poem say?"

Elvin took his hands off the crate to flip open the book. "It just says, 'tug its beard, and it will give you the key.'"

"Maybe something's supposed to happen with its mouth when you tug the beard." Alex tugged the beard once more and craned her neck back to look into the goat's mouth. "Wait a second, I think I see something. There's an opening in its mouth. It looks like someone just hammered out the concrete because it's really uneven." She stood on tiptoe so that she could slip her fingers into the jagged opening. As she did, her balance shifted and the crates toppled over. Alex landed hard, twisting her ankle in the process.

"Are you okay?" Jin rushed over to help.

Alex winced. "I'm fine. But thanks a lot, Elvin!

You were supposed to be holding the crates," she said as she rocked back and forth on the sidewalk, cradling her ankle.

"Sorry! I was looking at the book," Elvin apologized.

"I'll be right back," Jin said. She ran down to the bodega again and returned with a plastic bag filled with ice, which she handed to Alex. "Here, put this on your ankle," she said, and sat down beside her on the sidewalk. "Maybe we ought to call it quits for today."

"No way! We're too close to give up," Alex insisted. "The goat's mouth was empty, but it looked like someone could've taken something out before we got here."

"Maybe we have the wrong goat," Jin suggested. "What others do we know about?"

"What goat *don't* we know about?" Elvin quipped. "There's this one here. My grandfather was called the Goat. The goat was the original symbol of Harlem way back when. *The Life of the Invisibles* has one on its back cover. And last, but not least, there's the goat Pez dispenser that my grandfather gave me." Elvin took the toy out of his pocket. "My grandfather told me in the hospital that he hoped that the goat would tell me his story one day, but this thing never even worked."

"Halmoni wouldn't sell a broken Pez dispenser."

Jin grabbed the dispenser to inspect it. "See, some-thing's just jammed," she said, and gave the goat's beard a firm tug. The head flew off the dispenser, and a small metal object clattered to the sidewalk.

"The key!" Alex gasped.

"I guess that's what my grandfather meant about the goat telling me his story," Elvin surmised. "He must've taken it from the goat up there on the door and put it here for safekeeping when he saw Pugnacio and T.J. staking out the community garden. Maybe he thought that if they knew about the painting there, they might also discover the key."

"But we still don't know what the key opens," Alex pointed out.

"What does the poem say next?" Jin asked.

Elvin read the next lines of the poem. " 'To unlock the chamber where there once was peace without distinction, unity within difference.' "

Alex repeated several phrases aloud to herself, and then paused to think about them. "You know, the peace and unity parts kind of sound like what the Invisible 7 were all about," she said. "What if the chamber is literally the room where they came together?"

"And maybe the next part about the heart still beating is a metaphor for the paintings. The poem is saying that the paintings are alive, and they're waiting for us to uncover them, to remember them," Jin said excitedly.

"You could be right." Elvin flipped back to the first poem in the book. "It says, 'That which is invisible lives . . . visible to those who choose to see.'"

"I think this is it, guys! I think this is where the paintings are!" Alex leapt to her feet, immediately regretting it afterward, as sharp arrows of pain shot through her ankle.

"Alex, you are not okay. We need to take you to a doctor," Jin said, concerned.

"After we find the paintings," Alex said through clenched teeth.

"So if this is where the paintings are, how do we get inside?" Elvin asked, looking up at the abandoned building.

"Give me the key," Alex said. When Jin handed it over, Alex hobbled up to the front door to try the padlock. "No luck. We're going to have to break in. It's not like we haven't done it before." She winked.

"But the fire escape is on the front of this building. We'll never get away with it," argued Elvin.

"We'll just have to go around back." Alex started toward a chain-link fence on one side of the building. "There's a hole big enough to squeeze through here," she said.

Jin looked worried. "I don't like this. We don't know what's in there."

"I always carry pepper spray," Alex said, and pulled a small black aerosol can out of her pocket. "Besides, we're only going in to take a quick look."

After surveying the street for cops, she led the way through the chain-link fence to the back of the building. On the first floor, there were a few partially boarded-up windows. The wood on one of them was peeling back like it was about to fall off. Elvin reached up to jiggle the part that he could reach from the ground. "It's loose." It didn't take much to pry the old, weathered wood from the frame, exposing a partially broken window underneath. Elvin studied the window. "Brick," he said after a few minutes, like a surgeon ordering instruments during an operation.

Alex found one among the debris in the building's backyard. "Don't worry, I'll have my parents reimburse the owner for this," she told Jin, who looked like she was about to start hyperventilating.

She handed the brick to Elvin, who removed his coat and wrapped the brick inside. Then he swung it at the remaining glass, which fell away easily. He laid his coat across the bottom of the sill and slid through the window.

There was silence for what seemed like several long minutes.

"Are you all right in there?" Jin whispered loudly.

Elvin's head suddenly popped up in front of her. "All clear." The girls followed him through the window.

The air inside the building felt damp and smelled musty, like wet earth. Alex, Jin, and Elvin all switched on the flashlights on their phones and shined them around the room. They were in what used to be a kitchen, with a stove and a refrigerator still in place.

"Over there." Alex pointed toward a doorway that led to a narrow hall. They walked down the hall, pushing aside cobwebs and ignoring the sound of scurrying creatures at their feet, until they got to a closed door at the end. Alex, pepper spray at the ready, gave the door a light push and it squeaked open.

On the other side was a large, open room, lit by streaks of sunlight squeezing through the cracks in the boards on the windows. The room was empty except for a few padded chairs, a small desk in one corner, and a raised platform with a couple of thin pillars stretching from floor to ceiling at the front of the room.

"This must be where the church congregation that used to be here held their services," Jin observed.

"And before that, where the Invisible 7 held their

meetings." Alex looked around. "Read the next lines of the poem, Elvin."

" 'Encased in this place, my heart still beats, faint as an ember,' " Elvin read.

Alex shook her head. "What I don't get is the 'encased' part. If something is encased, it's enclosed in something, right? And ember, that makes me think of fire . . ." She wandered around the room, turning the lines over in her head.

"Look." Jin pointed. A plywood board, just a little taller than the desk, leaned against the wall. It didn't seem to fit in.

"Let's see if there's anything behind it," Alex said, and the three of them pushed the desk aside. The board fell to the floor without the support of the desk, revealing the hearth of a fireplace.

"The ember . . ." Alex muttered. She ignored the excruciating pain in her ankle and dropped to the floor to take a closer look. Sticking her head into the shallow opening, she could see that the back of the hearth was smooth, cold metal. "That's weird," she said to herself. She would've expected it to be brick or stone. She shined her light around, searching for anything that would tell her they were on the right track. And then she saw it. A small keyhole. She turned to her friends. "I need the key. Quick!"

Jin passed it over. Even before she tried it, Alex knew that it would fit.

They had found Henriette's paintings.

It took longer than they would have thought to empty the fireplace. It looked deceptively small from the outside, but inside Alex found canvases of all shapes and sizes, wrapped and rolled and boxed. While she worked them free of their hiding spot, Elvin and Jin laid each one out and tried not to let their mouths hang open. There were about thirty paintings in all.

"I think this is the last one," Alex said as she passed a small canvas out to Elvin.

Except it wasn't Elvin who took it from her, it was T.J.

"Let me give you a hand." T.J. grabbed her arm and dragged her up from the floor.

"Be careful. She's hurt!" Jin shouted.

Alex turned to see that Pugnacio and Clarence had already grabbed Jin and Elvin. Instinctively, Alex reached into her pocket for her pepper spray, but her hands were shaking so much, the can slipped out of her grasp and tumbled to the floor.

"Pepper spray, how cute." T.J. kicked the canister so hard, it rolled across the room to the doorway.

"Come on, let's deal with our little detectives here so that we can get out of this dump," Clarence said. "This place brings back bad memories."

T.J. produced a length of rope, and the men used it to roughly tie Jin and Alex to one of the pillars, Elvin to the other. Then Pugnacio stood watch while Clarence and T.J. started to load the paintings into rolling crates that they had waiting in the next room. They'd obviously planned ahead.

"Isn't this an appropriate end for a harrowing journey?" Pugnacio sneered, pacing in front of them. "Sacrificial lambs on the altar."

"How did you find us?" Elvin asked.

"Oh, T.J. followed you. He was at the museum today to resolve our little situation with Verta Mae Sneed, when you three showed up. We couldn't let such a bountiful opportunity pass—you've gotten so good at asking the right questions after all, and we can't have you spilling any of our secrets to the police. Councilman Markum pays us too well for that. So we decided to eliminate you three today instead. Verta Mae owes you a debt of gratitude. You saved her life— at least for the moment. Too bad she won't get a chance to thank you." Pugnacio grinned and lifted a jug of gasoline that the kids hadn't noticed. "It's a shame how people let these beautiful old buildings deteriorate. It's so easy for them to catch fire," he clucked.

Pugnacio began to pace. While his back was turned, Elvin kicked the pillar to get Jin and Alex's attention. He lifted his hands, which were tied behind him, to show them that he was working on untangling the knot. The girls nodded.

Just then, Clarence returned. As he picked up the last of the paintings to carry away, Alex called out to him.

"She didn't ruin your life, you know."

Clarence whirled around to face her. "What did you say?"

"I said, 'She didn't ruin your life.' It wasn't Henriette's fault that you gave up your dream of becoming an artist."

Clarence stormed up to the platform and grabbed Alex's jacket collar. "What do you know about it?" he yelled, spittle flying. "I gave my life to the Invisible 7, and Henriette selfishly dashed it all away. Like my life was worth nothing, like I was just a tool to be discarded once I'd outgrown my usefulness . . ."

"Pop, let's stay focused." Pugnacio firmly pulled his father away. "We have the paintings. Once we hand them over to Markum, he'll make us an important part of the Harlem World leadership. We'll be rid of these annoying runts and Verta Mae soon enough. This will all be over after today. Then you can finally move on with your life."

Clarence nodded and took a deep breath. "You're right, son," he said as he headed toward the door.

"Why don't you tell your dad what you really plan to do with the paintings once you get them out of here," Jin said loudly.

"You keep your mouth shut," Pugnacio hissed. He jumped onto the platform and squeezed Jin's arm so tightly, Alex could see tears forming in the corners of her eyes.

"Let her go!" Alex shouted as Clarence reappeared in the doorway.

"What's that about the paintings?" He eyed his son suspiciously.

"Nothing, Pop. These foolish children are just trying to make trouble," Pugnacio said, sheepishly.

"Tell him about your side deal with Markum, how he's actually going to make *you* the head of the new Harlem World art museum," Alex said.

Clarence's face contorted into an expression somewhere between rage and sorrow. For a second, Alex thought that he might cry. "Not you, too!"

Clarence shook his head sadly. "How could you betray me like this, after all that I've been through?"

"Pop, I'm sorry, but this is a good opportunity for me. Let's face it, you're old now. Your generation already had its chance." Pugnacio shrugged.

Clarence let out a deep, guttural roar. "I won't let this happen again. You're not going to take this opportunity away from me!" He dropped the paintings he was carrying and lunged toward Pugnacio, grabbing him around the neck.

While the two men struggled, Elvin released himself from the pillar and ran toward the can of pepper spray by the doorway. But before he could grab it, he saw something that had him reaching for the sky.

T.J. stood in the doorframe holding a gun. Shocked, Clarence and Pugnacio stopped fighting. T.J. nodded at the last of the paintings lying at their feet. They'd almost been trampled in the two men's scuffle. "Not cool, homeys," T.J. said, eyes darting from Pugnacio and Clarence to Elvin.

"I thought we said no weapons. They're too easily traced. These kids aren't worth going to jail over," Clarence said.

"I didn't bring it for them," T.J. said, waving the gun. "I brought it for you two."

"For us? Why?" Pugnacio asked.

"Just in case you tried to give me any trouble when I walk out of here with the paintings. Without you."

"What are you talking about, T.J.?" Clarence asked.

"I'm talking about the future, homey," T.J. said, casually. "While you two have been stuck in the past, I've been making moves with Markum. We agreed a long time ago that I would be the one to run the Harlem World art museum. All of that talk about history and preservation, that's just static, noise. This world belongs to the young, and I have the vision that's going to move this project forward."

T.J. pushed Elvin back onto the platform with Alex and Jin, and then pointed the gun at Clarence and Pugnacio, nodding for them to join the three kids. Keeping his gun trained on all of them, he grabbed the remaining canvases and smiled. "Thanks for the paintings," he said, the gun still pointed at them as he backed toward the kitchen.

Suddenly, a loud *boom* shook the walls. Armed police officers poured into the building from all directions.

"Drop your weapon!" several officers shouted. T.J. dropped the gun and fell to the floor. A throng of policemen descended on him, handcuffing him and dragging him away.

"Don't forget those two," a familiar voice rose above the din. Alex looked through the crowd of police to find Verta Mae Sneed standing behind the officers, pointing a finger squarely at Clarence and Pugnacio.

"I told you T.J. couldn't be trusted. Why don't you ever listen?"

"If you hadn't wasted time arguing with those kids, none of this would've happened!" Pugnacio and Clarence bickered as the police led them away.

When it was all over, Verta Mae flagged down a black livery car and squeezed into the backseat with Jin, Alex, and Elvin. Dr. Sneed directed the car to take them all to Harlem Hospital so that Elvin could see his grandfather, who had been very worried about him. Then she demanded a full account of their activities and was surprised to hear about how many people had helped them track down Henriette's legacy. Dr. Sneed had already contacted Alex and Jin's families, who were also on their way to meet the group. Jin thought that Rose and Rad should be there, too, so she texted them both an invitation. Rose texted back that she had some big news, but before Jin could ask what it was, Verta Mae cleared her throat.

"You children did a very dangerous thing today. You shouldn't have risked your lives like that. But you have done a tremendous service to the legacy of the Invisible 7 and to the great neighborhood of Harlem. I will communicate that to your families and plead for lenience on your behalf." She smiled then—for the first time since they'd met her, Jin noted.

"So how did you find us?" Elvin asked.

"Your grandfather called me. He thought that you might be on the hunt for the paintings, and told me that he believed Henriette had left clues to their whereabouts in a little book she'd written for all of us Invisibles. We went through my copy and were able to put the pieces together. Funny, I had forgotten all about that book."

Elvin was shocked. His grandfather *hadn't* written *The Life of the Invisibles* after all. It was kind of disappointing. He'd started to see the book as his grandfather's way of talking to him and teaching him about this special place. But now that Jacob was awake, maybe Elvin didn't need it anymore. He had the real thing. And knowing what he knew about Henriette and how she worked her invisible magic, maybe that was the point all along.

CHAPTER 23

SIX MONTHS LATER...

Alex, Jin, and Elvin wove their way through the steady stream of people on 125th Street, which was crowded even on a cold evening in February. The three were silent as they walked, curling up into their own thoughts, a small buffer against the frigid air, which settled around their shoulders like an icy shawl.

Since we rescued Henriette's paintings, so much has changed, Alex thought. Her father had admitted that even considering getting involved with Councilman Markum's Harlem World project had been a mistake. And when he'd finally listened to what Alex had to say about what the development was doing to their community, he'd gone a step further and figured out a way to shut the whole thing down. It turned out that many of the properties on Markum's demolition list were eligible to be designated as landmarks. And once an important real estate magnate like Rich Roebuck got involved, applications were quickly approved, the Harlem World project was scrapped, and Markum's career as a councilman was officially over.

Alex had even started helping out at her dad's company, coming up with ways to allow community members to be more involved in new development projects. She'd been thinking a lot about choices lately. About how people and communities deserved the right to make choices about their lives and neighborhoods. And about people whose power of choice had been taken away, and how she could help them get it back.

She even thought about her own choices. She remembered something that her dad had told her at the hospital after they'd found the paintings. She'd wanted him to promise that he'd only take on projects that wouldn't cause anyone to lose their homes or businesses. But while he had promised to think more carefully about the impact of his work, he'd also made some good points about how choosing one thing usually meant letting something else go.

Several months ago, on this very street, Alex had chosen to let Jin come with her to deliver food to a shelter. She hadn't wanted to do it because she was afraid of losing her independence and her strong will, qualities that she really liked about herself. Glancing over at Elvin and Jin, Alex realized that what she'd really let go of was the fear that no one would like her for who she was. She'd let down the walls she'd built up around herself and, as a result, gained two great new friends.

Jin caught Alex's eye and smiled. A few months ago, Jin had wondered whether or not they'd all still be friends after they found the paintings, but now she could see that she needn't have worried. Even without a mystery to solve, the three of them still hung out together all the time, and they were closer now than ever. Elvin had even moved in with the Roebucks until his grandfather was well enough to leave the hospital.

Still, Jin was hoping for a new mystery, a new puzzle to solve. She had been born and raised in Harlem, but meeting Alex and Elvin and learning about the Invisible 7 had helped her to see her neighborhood in a whole new way. She'd always been observant, but now everywhere she looked, she saw the story beneath the surface—in the harried faces of customers who came to her grandparents' store, in the pride of a flower box on a rusted fire escape, in the vacant lots that stood out like missing teeth, and even in the shiny new structures that seemed to sprout up overnight to fill the gaps. And she wanted to discover all their secrets.

Elvin gathered his grandfather's coat tightly around his body. It really wasn't heavy enough for the winter, but he'd gotten accustomed to wearing it, so he just put on several layers of clothes underneath. Besides, it had kind of become his good-luck charm. As they continued on, Elvin wove through the maze of people and swerved around bags of trash piled on the sidewalk near the curb like it was second nature. In fact, just a couple of days ago, he and Rad had skateboarded down this very street. It was hard at first to avoid crashing, but eventually he got the hang of it. He was getting used to this city.

When he first got to New York, he felt like he had landed on another planet, a loud and dirty one, where everything and everyone moved fast. Elvin had always been afraid that he'd disappear, get swallowed up by the enormity of the city. But looking for the paintings had helped him to break it down into manageable pieces. Now he could find his rhythm, his own places and spaces in the vastness. Suddenly, the streets and the houses and the people didn't seem so strange anymore. They were even starting to feel like home.

"We've got to hurry if we don't want to be late,"

Alex said as they picked up the pace and hoofed it the remaining blocks to the Studio Museum in Harlem. When they arrived, they spotted Rose and Rad in the crowd of people already gathered at the entrance.

"Hey, dudes!" Rad, who was actually wearing a suit, waved Alex, Jin, and Elvin over. "Verta Mae said for us to come in as soon as you guys got here. She's planned a special VIP tour of the new gallery for us."

The five of them walked up to the Verta Mae look-alike with the clipboard, who was checking off names at the door.

Just as Alex was steeling herself for a fight with the uptight administrator, a deep voice cut through the din of the crowd. "They're with me!" Verta Mae suddenly appeared behind the woman, who reluctantly let them in.

"I wanted you children to be the first to see the fruits of your labor," Verta Mae gushed as she led them into the museum. She stopped in front of the entrance to a gallery, so new that a faint smell of paint still hung in the air.

"Welcome to the newest addition to the Studio Museum. The Henriette Drummond Gallery. Thanks to the generous support of Alex's family, we were able to build an entire new wing of the museum, where Henriette's paintings will be on permanent display.

This gallery will be a space where young artists, especially those who are involved with the community, can display their work. There are also rooms set aside where Harlem residents and organizations can meet to plan community events," Verta Mae explained. "None of this would have been possible without you," she said, and, to everyone's surprise, gave each of them a big hug. "Now, have a quick look around before we have to let everyone else in."

"So you knew about this?" Jin whispered to Alex as they headed into the gallery.

Alex grinned and nodded. "But my parents swore me to secrecy. Isn't it amazing?" She marveled. *For once, having money isn't so bad,* she thought.

"It is amazing," Jin agreed. The walls of the gallery were white silhouettes in the shape of brownstones and storefronts, just like those on a typical Harlem block. On the walls hung Henriette's paintings, positioned where the windows and doors would be.

"They're beautiful," Jin whispered as she wandered through the gallery, taking in the paintings, which depicted scenes of life in Harlem and portraits of everyday people. So much had happened on the day that they found the paintings that she, Alex, and Elvin had not even had the chance to look at them.

"Guys, come take a look at this!" Elvin called

from the other side of the gallery. Alex and Jin walked over to where Elvin was standing in front of a small painting, perched in a first floor window. It was a portrait of a woman in coveralls with two, thick dark brown braids hanging on either side of her face.

"I think this is her. I think this is Henriette," Elvin whispered. The woman gazed back at them from the canvas, her brown eyes gleaming like polished glass.

"She looks sad," Alex commented, studying her face.

"No." Jin leaned in closer. "I think she's actually smiling."

In the few seconds that they'd been standing there, the edges of the woman's mouth seemed to curl into a mysterious smile.

"Yeah, I think you're right. She's smiling at us," Alex agreed. "I think she's happy that her paintings have finally found a home."

A few minutes later, people started to trickle into the gallery. Elvin spotted his grandfather and rushed over to meet him. Elvin's mother walked alongside Jacob, holding his arm for support. She was still recovering, but a few weeks earlier, the doctors in California had declared her stable enough to travel, and just that morning she'd told Elvin some big news. He waved his friends over.

"I want to introduce you guys to my mom," Elvin said proudly. "She's decided to move her treatments to Harlem Hospital. Which means I'm staying. We are officially New Yorkers!"

"Awesome, dude!" Rad reached out for a fist bump. "Now you can finally teach me how to do that noseslide move you've been working on."

Just then they heard a yelp. "Was that a dog?" Alex asked, looking around.

Rose nodded and squealed, then ran to meet Isabel, who had just come into the gallery. In her arms, she carried Noodles, Rose's beloved pug, who was all dressed up for the occasion in a dapper three-piece gray suit and doggy top hat, with space cut out for his ears.

"Does this mean . . . ?" Alex started.

Rose and Jin smiled at each other and nodded. "After we met Isabel, Jin and I thought that she would be the perfect new owner for Noodles," Rose explained. "Isabel agreed and adopted him! I not only get to see him whenever I want, but Isabel has also become my fashion mentor. We designed the outfit Noodles is wearing together," Rose gushed.

"Sounds perfect. I'm happy Noodles found a good home, and I mean that." Alex smiled.

"May I have your attention please?" Verta Mae stood at the front of the room with a microphone. Once the crowd had quieted down, she welcomed everyone and told them about the significance of the gallery and Henriette's paintings. She even invited Elvin's grandfather and Isabel up to talk about the history of the Invisible 7.

At the end of the presentation, she thanked Alex's parents and then turned to Elvin, Jin, Alex, Rose, and Rad. "We would not be standing here in this beautiful new space were it not for the bravery and commitment of these young people," Verta Mae said, and introduced each of them. The room practically shook with applause and cheers. Verta Mae raised her hands for quiet.

"We are dedicating this space to all of them," she said. Then she held up a gold-plated plaque on which each of their names was engraved. "We are also including this statement, authored by Jin Yi and Alex Roebuck, as part of the permanent exhibit of Henriette's paintings."

Jin and Alex's jaws dropped as Verta Mae unveiled a large white canvas, on which an excerpt from their history project was printed. When Verta Mae found out that they had chosen to research and write about Harlem World and the Invisible 7, she had asked to read their paper. They had no idea that she planned to include it in an actual art exhibition.

"Girls, please come up and share this with our audience. I think we'd all like to hear this read in your own voices," Verta Mae urged.

Nervously, Alex and Jin walked to the front of the room and took turns reading aloud the concluding statement of their project, which they had written together.

> *"Art is a mirror that reflects who we are, and who we hope to be. It can expose evil, greed, and war, but it can also illuminate love, joy, and unity.*
>
> *Art can reveal the mistakes of the past and also help us to discover a path to forgiveness and healing.*
>
> *For many years, Harlem artists like Henriette Drummond and the members of the Invisible 7 have used art to tell the stories that they felt were important to tell.*
>
> *Their art asks the questions 'Who are you? How do you want to see yourself reflected?'*
>
> *Art gives us the choice, and with it, a way to tell our own stories and to shape our own futures."*

Alex and Jin were stunned by the thundering applause that followed. They shuffled back toward their families, and soon the celebratory gala was in full swing.

As Jin glanced around the room at her friends and neighbors, she saw the true power of art on full display. Mr. and Mrs. Roebuck stood with Harabeoji in front of a particularly incredible painting that showed neighborhood commerce at work. Elvin and Rad were huddled deep in conversation with Elvin's grandfather. Rose was talking to Verta Mae Sneed, of all people. It must have been about something fashion-related, because she had whipped out her tape measure and was measuring Verta Mae's arms and shoulders. And Alex and Elvin's mother were laughing uproariously, at what Jin could only imagine. The scene reminded Jin of another of Henriette's paintings, the mural that depicted a group of neighbors gathered together and enjoying one another on a block in Harlem.

Then she noticed her grandmother, standing off by herself, in front of Henriette's self-portrait. As Jin headed toward her, she saw Halmoni dab at her eyes with a tissue—she was crying!

"Halmoni! Are you okay?"

Halmoni reached for Jin and pulled her into a hug. "I'm just happy." She beamed. "And so proud of you,

Jinnie. You and your friends, you bring our neighborhood together again. You stand up for Harlem. You
tough, like me."

Jin felt her own tears welling up at that moment.
She'd always admired her grandmother's strength—
even if it meant Halmoni could be harsh at times.
And it meant a lot for Halmoni to say that Jin was
tough like her. It was like she was seeing Halmoni in
a whole new way, shifting the perspective as Elvin's
mother said. Jin usually focused on her grandmother's
strictness and fussiness, but she realized now, her
grandmother had a softness and kindness that had
also been there all along. Halmoni had given Jin the
space to go on this adventure with Elvin and Alex,
while still making her feel safe and protected.

Art really can bring people together. Jin smiled to
herself and leaned into her grandmother's warm
embrace.

AUTHOR'S NOTE

In *The Harlem Charade,* characters attempt to unravel the truth about the past, while asking some very important questions about the future like, Who gets to decide what is important about a community? How can people embrace the future without completely losing the past? Who gets to tell our stories?

This book takes place in Harlem, a neighborhood in New York City, well known as a mecca of African American arts, culture, and history. The people and events as described in the story are fictional, but it is a fact that the Harlem community has experienced tremendous growth and change. This change has brought new restaurants, apartment and entertainment complexes, stores, and residents to the area, but it has also resulted in the disappearance of local small businesses and other sites, many of which had historical significance to the neighborhood.

Nearly fifty years ago, a group of Harlem residents and artists were grappling with many of these same issues of change and representation. In 1969, the Metropolitan Museum of Art mounted an exhibit entitled, *Harlem on My Mind: Cultural Capital of Black America, 1900–1968,* which you will find referenced in this book. Coming on the heels of the Civil Rights Movement, the exhibit sought to explore the culture and history of Harlem's predominantly black community.

Though on the surface, *Harlem on My Mind* may have seemed like a good idea, the exhibit actually sparked intense controversy, debate, and division among artists and curators of the show. Harlem artists, whose work at that time was already underrepresented in galleries and museums in New York and around the country, were infuriated by the lack of input that actual Harlem residents had in the planning of *Harlem on My Mind*. They also resented the Met's decision to include only photography in the exhibit—which excluded painters and artists working in other mediums.

Artists, like the fictional characters of Henriette Drummond and the Invisible 7 in this story, launched heated protests against the show, the most serious of which resulted in the vandalism of several paintings in the Metropolitan Museum's collection. These artists were fighting not just for the right to exhibit their work but also for the right to represent themselves and their community: to tell their stories.

Fortunately, this story has a somewhat happy ending. As a result of Harlem artists protesting and raising questions in the 1960s, many museums and galleries began to increase efforts to exhibit and collect art by a more diverse array of artists. In addition, new institutions, like the Studio Museum in Harlem, were founded and continue today to be devoted to the exhibition and development of work by artists of color.

Still, there is work to be done. The writer Toni Morrison said, "Writers are like [water]: remembering where we were . . . the light that was there and the route back to our original place. It is emotional memory—what the nerves and the skin remember as well as how it appeared. And a rush of imagination is our 'flooding.'"

I believe she's saying that remembering the past is how we see who we really are. It is our job as writers, readers, students, teachers, and community members, to seek out and excavate memories of the past, which still live buried beneath all the shiny newness, then weave them into our visions for the future. It is our job to remember, to tell our truths and our stories.

A NOTE ON EVENTS AND LOCATIONS IN THE BOOK

All events and characters in this book are fictional. However, I did use some real events and locations in the story. I took artistic license with some of the locations in the book, but I do hope that you will visit these places, read more about these events, and explore them on your own.

1. The Metropolitan Museum of Art (the Met) is one of the world's most highly regarded art museums. It is located on Fifth Avenue in New York City.

2. The exhibition, *Harlem on My Mind: Cultural Capital of Black America, 1900–1968* was shown at the Met in 1969. Ten paintings in the museum's collection were vandalized in protest of the *Harlem on My Mind* exhibit, though authorities never found the person(s) who did it.

3. The Studio Museum in Harlem is an actual museum, located on historic 125th Street.

It was one of the institutions founded as a result of the dialogue and debate about art and representation that was sparked by the *Harlem on My Mind* exhibit.

4. Harlem Hospital (Harlem Hospital Center) is an actual hospital in Harlem, located on 135th Street and Malcolm X Boulevard, also known as Lenox Avenue. It is home to several historically significant murals painted by artists Vertis Hayes and Georgette Seabrook, among others, during the 1930s as part of the Federal Works Progress Administration program. These murals, and the real controversy that surrounded them, were the inspiration for the murals in this story. You can see the original restored murals on display in the Mural Pavilion at the Harlem Hospital Center, and read more about them here: http://www.nytimes.com/2012/09/17/arts/design/murals-at-harlem-hospital-get-a-new-life.html?_r=0.

5. The Schomburg Center for Research in Black Culture is a research library that is

home to one of the country's most significant collections of materials about the lives and experiences of people of African descent. It is also located on the corner of 135th Street and Malcolm X Boulevard in Harlem and is part of the New York Public Library system.

6. The Magic Skillet is a fictional establishment, based on the real Harlem restaurant, Pan-Pan. Pan-Pan was located on the corner of 135th Street and Malcolm X Boulevard, across the street from the Schomburg Center, but was destroyed in a fire in 2004.

7. As of this writing, there is a rare Victorian carriage house at 122nd Street and Seventh Avenue. Built as a private carriage house in the nineteenth century, this building is significant because there are few such structures still existing in Harlem. Residents are attempting to landmark this property in order to preserve it.

ACKNOWLEDGMENTS

Thank you to my superstar editor, Jenne Abramowitz, for believing in this project. Your keen insights and questions helped to bring out the heart of this story and shape it into an even better book. Thanks also to Andrea Davis Pinkney, Abby McAden, and the entire Scholastic team for welcoming me to the fold, and for ushering this book out into the world.

To my niece, Marianna Elise Tarpley, and my nephew, Sebastian Jonah Dennis Tarpley, who are constant sources of inspiration and my two best reasons to keep writing.

To my sisters, Elizabeth and Nicole Tarpley, and to my brother, Omar Tarpley: Thank you for your constant support. It has meant so much to me in more ways than you know.

To my extended family—my mother-in-law, Adeline Féthière; Germaine "Tante Gette" Charlier; my sister- and brother-in-law, Sabine and Gunter Berding: Thank you for welcoming me into your family and for providing delicious meals during the writing of this book—not to mention, the opportunity to practice my French and German.

To Galen "Pen" Pendelton, one of my closest

friends—and also my running coach: Thank you for your many words of wisdom, for staying on me to "finish the book," and for reminding me that I am a "marathon woman."

To my friend and former professor, Len Rubinowitz: Thank you for supporting my work all these years, and for the shelf in your office reserved for my books.

And to my friends (and neighbors) Bernadette Tucker Duck, Rachel Gregersen, and Jane and Bob Bushwaller: Thank you for your enthusiastic support of my work and for making me feel at home in our neighborhood.

To Gloria and Al Needlman: Thank you for being a source of encouragement, creativity, and inspiration for me and so many others who were lucky enough to be in your classroom (Gloria) and home, and for introducing me to my *beschert*.

To my mom, Marlene Tarpley, my best friend, who has read every word: Thank you for always encouraging and nurturing my curiosity and creativity, and for the books and stories in our home that began my writing adventure.

To my husband, Claude Féthière: Thank you for the joy and laughter, the '80s music sing-alongs, and impromptu kitchen dances that you bring into my life. I appreciate the many things that you do to take care of me and our family, which have made it possible for me to continue to do the work that I love.

To my "kittos" Manhattan and Summer, who kept me company during the writing of this book and all the others. I love and miss you both.

ABOUT THE AUTHOR

Natasha Tarpley is the author of the bestselling picture book *I Love My Hair!* and other acclaimed titles for children and adults. She is the recipient of a National Endowment for the Arts fellowship, among other awards. When she is not writing books, Ms. Tarpley can usually be found reading them. She has also taken up the cruel and unusual hobby of running marathons. Ms. Tarpley is the cofounder of Voonderbar! Media, a multicultural children's book publishing and media company. She fell in love with Harlem and New York City and lived there for many years before moving back to her hometown of Chicago, Illinois, where she lives with her husband and works alongside her neighbors to make their community a better place.